DARK ENTRIES

Dark Entries

ROBERT AICKMAN

FABER & FABER

First published in this edition in 2014
by Faber & Faber Limited
The Bindery, 51 Hatton Garden
London ECIN 8HN

Typeset by by Faber & Faber Limited
Printed and bound by CPI Group (UK) Ltd, Croydon, CRO 4YY

Ramsey Campbell's 'Robert Remembered' first appeared in a shorter
form in *Night Voices*, published in 2013 by Tartarus Press

The right of Robert Aickman to be identified as author of this work has
been asserted in accordance with Section 77 of the Copyright, Designs and
Patents Act 1988

A CIP record for this book is available from the British Library

ISBN 978-0-571-31177-4

For
GEORGIA
Dauphine de Lyonnesse

Contents

Robert Aickman: An Introduction

by Richard T. Kelly

Is Robert Fordyce Aickman (1914–81) the twentieth century's 'most profound writer of what we call horror stories and he, with greater accuracy, preferred to call strange stories'? Such was the view of Peter Straub, voiced in a discerning introduction to Aickman's posthumous collection *The Wine-Dark Sea*. If you grant Aickman his characteristic insistence on self-classification within this genre of 'strange', then you might say he was in a league of his own (rather as Edgar Allan Poe is the lone and undisputed heavyweight in the field of 'tales of mystery and imagination'). 'Horror', though, is clearly the most compelling genre label that exists on the dark side of literary endeavour. So it might be simplest and most useful to the cause of extending Aickman's fame if we agree that, yes, he was the finest horror writer of the last hundred years.

So elegantly and comprehensively does Aickman encompass all the traditional strengths and available complexities of the supernatural story that, at times, it's hard to see how any subsequent practitioner could stand anywhere but in his shadow. True, there is perhaps a typical Aickman protagonist – usually but not always a man, and one who does not fit so well with others, temperamentally inclined to his own company. But Aickman has a considerable gift for putting us stealthily behind the eyes of said protagonist. Having established such identification, the way in which he then builds up a sense of dread is masterly. His construction of sentences and of narrative is patient and finical. He seems always to proceed from a rather grey-toned realism where detail accumulates without fuss, and the recognisable material world appears wholly four-square – until you realise that the narrative has been built as a cage, a kind of personal hell, and our protagonist is walking toward death as if in a dream.

This effect is especially pronounced – Aickman, as it were, preordains the final black flourish – in stories such as 'Never Visit Venice' (the title gives the nod) and 'The Fetch', whose confessional protagonist rightly judges himself 'a haunted man', his pursuer a grim and faceless wraith who emerges from the sea periodically to augur a death in the family. Sometimes, though, to paraphrase John Donne, the Aickman protagonist runs to death just as fast as death can meet him: as in 'The Stains', an account of a scholarly widower's falling in love with – and plunging to his undoing through – a winsome young woman who is, in fact, some kind of dryad.

On this latter score it should be said that, for all Aickman's seeming astringency, many of his stories possess a powerful erotic charge. There is, again, something dreamlike to how quickly in Aickman an attraction can proceed to a physical expression; and yet he also creates a deep unease whenever skin touches skin – as if desire (and the feminine) are forms of snare, varieties of doom. If such a tendency smacks rather of neurosis, one has to say that this is where a great deal of horror comes from; and Aickman carries off his version of it with great panache, always.

On the flipside of the coin one should also acknowledge Aickman's refined facility for writing female protagonists, and that the ambience of such tales – the world they conjure, the character's relations to people and things in that world – is highly distinctive and noteworthy within his *oeuvre*. Aickman's women are generally spared the sort of grisly fates he reserves for his men, and yet still he routinely leaves us to wonder if they are headed to heaven or hell, if not confined to some purgatory. Among his most admired stories in this line are 'The Inner Room' and 'Into the Wood', works in which the mystery deepens upon the final sentence.

And lest we forget: Aickman can be very witty, too, even in the midst of mounting horrors, and even if it's laughter in the dark. English readers in particular tend to chuckle over 'The Hospice', the story of a travelling salesman trapped in his worst nightmare of a guesthouse, where the guests are kept in ankle-fetters and the evening meal is served in mountainous indigestible heaps ('It's turkey tonight . . .'). In the aforementioned 'The Fetch', when our haunted man finally finds himself caged in his Scottish family home, watching the wraith watching him from a perch outdoors up high on a broken wall, he still has time to reflect that 'such levitations are said to be not uncommon in the remoter parts of Scotland'. This is the sound of a refined intellect, an author amusing both himself and us.

2014 is the centenary of Aickman's birth and sees him honoured at the annual World Fantasy Convention, the forum where, in 1975, his story 'Pages from a Young Girl's Journal' received the award for short fiction. His cult has been secure since then, and yet those who have newly discovered his rare brilliance have quite often wondered why he is not better known outside the supernatural cognoscenti.

One likely reason is that his body of work is so modestly sized: there are only forty-eight extant 'strange stories', and there was never a novel; or, to be precise, the two longer-form Aickmans that have been published – *The Late Breakfasters* in 1964 and *The Model*, posthumously, in 1987 – were fantastical (the latter especially), not to say exquisite, but had nothing overtly eerie or blood-freezing about them. Aickman simply refused to cash in on his most marketable skills as a writer (somewhat to the chagrin of the literary agents who represented him).

He was also a relatively late starter. *We Are for the Dark*, his co-publication with Elizabeth Jane Howard to which they contributed three tales apiece, appeared from Jonathan Cape in 1951; but nothing followed until 1964, with his first discrete collection, *Dark Entries*. By the turn of the 1980s he was a significant figure in the landscape, and from there his renown might have widened. It was then, however, that he developed the cancer from which he would die, on 26 February 1981, having refused chemotherapy in favour of homeopathic treatments.

Aickman's name would surely enjoy a wider currency today if any of his works had been adapted for cinema, a medium of which he was a discerning fan. And yet, to date, no such adaptation has come about. If we agree that a masterpiece is an idea expressed in its perfect creative form then it may be fair to say that the perfection Aickman achieved in the short story would not suffer to be stretched to ninety minutes or more across a movie screen. But the possibility still exists, for sure. If Aickman made a frightening world all of his own on the page, he also took on some of the great and familiar horror tropes, and treated them superbly.

To wit: the classic second piece in *Dark Entries*, 'Ringing the Changes', is a zombie story, immeasurably more ghastly and nerve-straining than *The Walking Dead*. And the aforementioned 'Pages from a Young Girl's Journal' is a vampire story, concerning a pubescent girl bored rigid by her family's Grand Tour of Italy in 1815, until she is pleasurably transformed by an encounter with a tall, dark, sharp-toothed stranger. In other words it is about the empowering effects of blood-sucking upon adolescent girls; and worth ten of the *Twilight*s of this world. On the strength of such accomplishments one can see that, while Aickman remains for the moment a cult figure, his stories retain the potential to reach many more new admirers far and wide – rather like the vampirised Jonathan Harker at the end of Werner Herzog's *Nosferatu the Vampyre* (1979), riding out on his steed to infect the world.

Had Aickman never written a word of fiction of his own he would still have a place in the annals of horror: a footnote, perhaps, to observe that he was the maternal grandson of Richard Marsh, bestselling sensational/supernatural novelist of the late-Victorian and Edwardian eras; but an extensive entry for his endeavours as an anthologist who helped to define a canon of supernatural fiction through his editing of the first eight volumes of the *Fontana Book of Great Ghost Stories* between 1964 and 1972.

His enduring reputation, though, would have been based on his co-founding in 1944 of the Inland Waterways Association, dedicated to the preservation and restoration of England's inland canals. Such a passionate calling might be considered perfect for an author of 'strange stories' – also for a man who was, in some profound way, out of step with or apart from his own time. By all accounts Aickman gave the IWA highly energetic leadership and built up its profile and activities with rigour and zeal. His insistent style, however, did not delight everyone: in 1951 he argued and fell out definitively with L. T. C. (Tom) Rolt, fellow conservationist and author, whose seminal book *Narrow Boat* (1944) had inspired the organisation's founding in the first place.

When we admire a writer we naturally wish to

know more of what they were like as a person. Aickman's admirers have sometimes found what they have heard of him to be a shade forbidding. Culturally he was a connoisseur who had highly finessing tastes in theatre, ballet, opera and classical music. Socially he was punctilious and fastidious, unabashedly erudite, an autodidact not shy about airing his education. His political instincts were conservative, his outlook elitist. The late Elizabeth Jane Howard – first secretary of the Inland Waterways Association, with whom Aickman fell in love and for whom he carried a torch years after her ending of their brief relationship – would tell an interviewer some years later that there were at least two sides to the man: 'He could be very prickly and difficult, or he could be very charming.'

Nonetheless, those whom Aickman allowed to know him well and whom he liked and trusted in turn clearly found him to be the most marvellous company – for a night at the theatre, say, or a visit to a rural stately home, or at a catered dinner *à deux*, after which he would be inclined to read aloud from whichever strange story he was then working on. The reader will learn more in this line from the afterwords to this series of Faber reissues, which have been written by admiring friends who had just such a privileged insight into the author.

These reissues are in honour of Aickman's 2014 centenary. Along with the present volume, readers may choose from *Cold Hand in Mine*, the posthumously published compilations *The Unsettled Dust* and *The Wine-Dark Sea*, and (as Faber Finds) *The Late Breakfasters* and

The Model. Whether these works are already known to you or you are about to discover them, the injunction is the same – prepare to be entranced, compelled, seduced, petrified.

RICHARD T. KELLY *is the author of the novels* Crusaders *and* The Possessions of Doctor Forrest.

The School Friend

'To be taken advantage of is every
woman's secret wish.'
Princess Elizabeth Bibesco

It would be false modesty to deny that Sally Tessler
and I were the bright girls of the school. Later it was
understood that I went more and more swiftly to the
bad; but Sally continued being bright for some considerable time. Like many males, but few females, even
among those inclined to scholarship, Sally combined a
true love for the Classics, the ancient ones, with an insight into mathematics which, to the small degree that
I was interested, seemed to me almost magical. She
won three scholarships, two gold medals, and a sojourn
among the Hellenes with all expenses paid. Before she
had graduated she had published a little book of popular
mathematics which, I understood, made her a surprising
sum of money. Later she edited several lesser Latin au-
thors, published in editions so small that they can have
brought her nothing but inner satisfaction.

The foundations of all this erudition had almost certainly been laid in Sally's earliest childhood. The tale
went that Dr Tessler had once been the victim of some
serious injustice, or considered that he had: certainly

it seemed to be true that, as his neighbours put it, he 'never went out'. Sally herself once told me that she not only could remember nothing of her mother, but had never come across any trace or record of her. From the very beginning Sally had been brought up, it was said, by her father alone. Rumour suggested that Dr Tessler's regimen was three-fold: reading, domestic drudgery, and obedience. I deduced that he used the last to enforce the two first: when Sally was not scrubbing the floor or washing up, she was studying Vergil and Euclid. Even then I suspected that the Doctor's ways of making his will felt would not have borne examination by the other parents. Certainly, however, when Sally first appeared at school, she had much more than a grounding in almost every subject taught, and in several which were not taught. Sally, therefore, was from the first a considerable irritant to the mistresses. She was always two years or more below the average age of her form. She had a real technique of acquiring knowledge. She respected learning in her preceptors, and detected its absence . . . I once tried to find out in what subject Dr Tessler had obtained his doctorate. I failed; but, of course, one then expected a German to be a doctor.

It was the first school Sally had attended. I was a member of the form to which she was originally assigned; but in which she remained for less than a week, so eclipsing to the rest of us was her mass of information. She was thirteen years and five months old at the time; nearly a year younger than I. (I owe it to myself to say that I was promoted at the end of the term; and thereafter more or less kept pace with the prodigy, although this, perhaps, was for special reasons.) Her hair was remarkably beautiful; a perfect light blonde, and lustrous with brushing, although cut short and 'done' in no particular way, indeed usually very untidy. She had dark eyes, a pale skin, a large distinguished nose, and a larger mouth. She had also a slim but precocious figure, which later put me in mind of Tessa in *The Constant Nymph*. For better or for worse, there was no school uniform, and Sally invariably appeared in a dark-blue dress of foreign aspect and extreme simplicity, which none the less distinctly became her looks. As she grew, she seemed to wear later editions of the same dress, new and enlarged, like certain publications.

Sally, in fact, was beautiful; but one would be unlikely ever to meet another so lovely who was so entirely and genuinely unaware of the fact and of its implications. And, of course, her casualness about her appearance, and her simple clothes, added to her charm. Her disposition seemed kindly and easy-going in the extreme; and her voice was lazy to drawling. But Sally, none the less, seemed to live only in order to work; and, although I was, I think, her closest friend (it was the urge to keep up with her which explained much of my own progress in the school), I learnt very little about her. She seemed to have no pocket-money at all: as this amounted to a social deficiency of the vastest magnitude, and as my parents could afford to be and were generous, I regularly shared with her. She accepted the arrangement simply and warmly. In return she gave me frequent little

3

presents of books: a copy of Goethe's *Faust* in the original language and bound in somewhat discouraging brown leather; and an edition of Petronius, with some remarkable drawings . . . Much later, when in need of money for a friend, I took the *Faust*, in no hopeful spirit, to Sotheby's. It proved to be a rebound first edition . . .

But it was a conversation about the illustrations in the Petronius (I was able to construe Latin fairly well for a girl, but the italics and long s's daunted me) which led me to the discovery that Sally knew more than any of us about the subject illustrated. Despite her startling range of information she seemed then, and certainly for long after, completely disinterested in any personal way. It was as if she discoursed, in the gentlest, sweetest manner, about some distant far-off thing, or, to use a comparison absurdly hackneyed but here appropriate, about botany. It was an ordinary enough school, and sex was a preoccupation among us. Sally's attitude was surprisingly new and unusual. In the end she did ask me not to tell the others what she had just told me.

'As if I would,' I replied challengingly, but still musingly.

And in fact I didn't tell anyone until considerably later: when I found that I had learned from Sally things which no one else at all seemed to know; things which I sometimes think have in themselves influenced my life, so to say, not a little. Once I tried to work out how old Sally was at the time of this conversation. I think she could hardly have been more than fifteen.

*

4

In the end Sally won her university scholarship, and I just failed, but won the school's English Essay Prize, and also the Good Conduct Medal, which I deemed (and still deem) in the nature of a stigma, but believed, consolingly, to be awarded more to my prosperous father than to me. Sally's conduct was in any case much better than mine, being indeed irreproachable. I had entered for the scholarship with the intention of forcing the examiners, in the unlikely event of my winning it, to bestow it upon Sally, who really needed it. When this doubtless impracticable scheme proved unnecessary, Sally and I parted company, she to her triumphs of the intellect, I to my lesser achievements. We corresponded intermittently, but decreasingly as our areas of common interest diminished. Ultimately, for a very considerable time, I lost sight of her altogether, although occasionally over the years I used to see reviews of her learned books, and encounter references to her in leading articles about the Classical Association and similar indispensable bodies. I took it for granted that by now we should have difficulty in communicating at all. I observed that Sally did not marry. One couldn't wonder, I foolishly and unkindly drifted into supposing . . .

When I was forty-one, two things happened which have a bearing on this narrative. The first was that a catastrophe befell me which led to my again taking up residence with my parents. Details are superfluous. The second thing was the death of Dr Tessler.

I should probably have heard of Dr Tessler's death in

any case, for my parents, who, like me and the rest of the neighbours, had never set eyes upon him, had always regarded him with mild curiosity. As it was, the first I knew of it was when I saw the funeral. I was shopping on behalf of my mother, and reflecting upon the vileness of things, when I observed old Mr Orbit remove his hat, in which he always served, and briefly sink his head in prayer. Between the aggregations of Shredded Wheat in the window, I saw the passing shape of a very old-fashioned and therefore very ornate horse-drawn hearse. It bore a coffin covered in a pall of worn purple velvet; but there seemed to be no mourners at all.

'Didn't think never to see a 'orse 'earse again, Mr Orbit,' remarked old Mrs Rind, who was ahead of me in the queue.

'Pauper funeral, I expect,' said her friend old Mrs Edge.

'No such thing no more,' said Mr Orbit quite sharply, and replacing his hat. 'That's Dr Tessler's funeral. Don't suppose 'e 'ad no family come to look after things.'

I believe the three white heads then got together, and began to whisper; but, on hearing the name, I had made towards the door. I looked out. The huge ancient hearse, complete with vast black plumes, looked much too big for the narrow autumnal street. It put me in mind of how toys are often so grossly out of scale with one another. I could now see that instead of mourners, a group of urchins, shadowy in the fading light, ran behind the bier, shrieking and jeering: a most regrettable scene in a well-conducted township.

6

For the first time in months, if not years, I wondered about Sally.

Three days later she appeared without warning at my parents' front door. It was I who opened it.

'Hallo, Mel.'

One hears of people who after many years take up a conversation as if the same number of hours had passed. This was a case in point. Sally, moreover, looked almost wholly unchanged. Possibly her lustrous hair was one half-shade darker, but it was still short and wild. Her lovely white skin was unwrinkled. Her large mouth smiled sweetly but, as always, somewhat absently. She was dressed in the most ordinary clothes, but still managed to look like anything but a don or a dominie: although neither did she look like a woman of the world. It was, I reflected, hard to decide what she did look like.

'Hallo, Sally.'

I kissed her and began to condole.

'Father really died before I was born. You know that.'

'I have heard something.' I should not have been sorry to hear more; but Sally threw off her coat, sank down before the fire, and said:

'I've read all your books. I loved them. I should have written.'

'Thank you,' I said. 'I wish there were more who felt like you.'

'You're an artist, Mel. You can't expect to be a success at the same time.' She was warming her white hands. I was not sure that I was an artist, but it was nice to be told.

There was a circle of leather-covered armchairs

7

round the fire. I sat down beside her. 'I've read about you often in the *Times Lit*,' I said, 'but that's all. For years. Much too long.'

'I'm glad you're still living here,' she replied.

'Not *still*. Again.'

'Oh?' She smiled in her gentle, absent way.

'Following a session in the frying-pan, and another one in the fire ... I'm sure you've been conducting yourself more sensibly.' I was still fishing.

But all she said was, 'Anyway I'm still glad you're living here.'

'Can't say *I* am. But why in particular?'

'Silly Mel! Because I'm going to live here too.'

I had never even thought of it.

I could not resist a direct question.

'Who told you your father was ill?'

'A friend. I've come all the way from Asia Minor. I've been looking at potsherds.' She was remarkably untanned for one who had been living under the sun; but her skin was of the kind which does not tan readily.

'It will be lovely to have you about again. Lovely, Sally. But what will you do here?'

'What do *you* do?'

'I write ... In other ways my life is rather over, I feel.'

'*I* write too. Sometimes. At least I edit ... And I don't think my life, properly speaking, has ever begun.'

I had spoken in self-pity, although I had not wholly meant to do so. The tone of her reply I found it impossible to define. Certainly, I thought with slight malice, certainly she does look absurdly virginal.

8

A week later a van arrived at Dr Tessler's house, containing a great number of books, a few packed trunks, and little else; and Sally moved in. She offered no further explanation for this gesture of semi-retirement from the gay world (for we lived about forty miles from London, too many for urban participation, too few for rural self-sufficiency); but it occurred to me that Sally's resources were doubtless not so large that she could disregard an opportunity to live rent-free, although I had no idea whether the house was freehold, and there was no mention even of a will. Sally was and always had been so vague about practicalities, that I was a little worried about these matters; but she declined ideas of help. There was no doubt that if she were to offer the house for sale, she could not expect from the proceeds an income big enough to enable her to live elsewhere; and I could imagine that she shrank from the bother and uncertainty of letting.

I heard about the contents of the van from Mr Ditch, the remover; and it was, in fact, not until she had been in residence for about ten days that Sally sent me an invitation. During this time, and after she had refused my help with her affairs, I had thought it best to leave her alone. Now, although the house which I must thenceforth think of as hers stood only about a quarter of a mile from the house of my parents, she sent me a postcard. It was a picture postcard of Mitylene. She asked me to tea.

The way was through the avenues and round the

corners of a mid-nineteenth-century housing estate for merchants and professional men. My parents' house was intended for the former; Sally's for the latter. It stood, in fact, at the very end of a cul-de-sac: even now the house opposite bore the plate of a dentist.

I had often stared at the house during Dr Tessler's occupancy, and before I knew Sally; but not until that day did I enter it. The outside looked much as it had ever done. The house was built in a grey brick so depressing that one speculated how anyone could ever come to choose it (as many once did, however, throughout the Home Counties). To the right of the front door (approached by twelve steps, with blue and white tessellated risers) protruded a greatly disproportionate obtuse-angled bay window: it resembled the thrusting nose on a grey and wrinkled face. This bay window served the basement, the ground floor, and the first floor: between the two latter ran a dull red string course 'in an acanthus pattern', like a chaplet round the temples of a dowager. From the second-floor window it might have been possible to step on to the top of the projecting bay, the better to view the surgery opposite; had not the second-floor window been barred, doubtless as protection for a nursery. The wooden gate had fallen from its hinges, and had to be lifted open and shut. It was startlingly heavy.

The bell was in order.

Sally was, of course, alone in the house.

Immediately she opened the door (which included two large tracts of coloured glass), I apprehended a change in her; essentially the first change in all the time I had known her, for the woman who had come to my parents' house a fortnight or three weeks before had seemed to me very much the girl who had joined my class when we were both children. But now there was a difference . . .

In the first place she looked different. Previously there had always been a distinction about her appearance, however inexpensive her clothes. Now she wore a fawn jumper which needed washing, and stained, creaseless grey slacks. When a woman wears trousers, they need to be smart. These were slacks indeed. Sally's hair was not so much picturesquely untidy as in the past, but, more truly, in bad need of trimming. She wore distasteful sandals. And her expression had altered.

'Hallo, Mel. Do you mind sitting down and waiting for the kettle to boil?' She showed me into the ground-floor room (although to make possible the basement, it was cocked high in the air) with the bay window. 'Just throw your coat on a chair.' She bustled precipitately away. It occurred to me that Sally's culinary aplomb had diminished since her busy childhood of legend.

The room was horrible. I had expected eccentricity, discomfort, bookworminess, even perhaps the slightly macabre. But the room was entirely commonplace, and in the most unpleasing fashion. The furniture had probably been mass-produced in the early twenties. It was of the kind which it is impossible, by any expenditure of time and polish, to keep in good order. The carpet was dingy jazz. There were soulless little pictures in gilt frames. There were dreadful modern knick-knacks. There was a wireless set, obviously long broken . . . For the time of year, the rickety, smoky fire offered none too much heat. Rejecting Sally's invitation, I drew my coat about me.

There was nothing to read except a pre-war copy of *Tit-Bits* which I found on the floor under the lumpy settee. Like Sally's jumper, the dense lace curtains could have done with a wash. But before long Sally appeared with tea: six uniform pink cakes from the nearest shop, and a flavourless liquid full of floating 'strangers'. The crockery accorded with the other appurtenances.

I asked Sally whether she had started work of any kind.

'Not yet,' she replied, a little dourly. 'I've got to get things going in the house first.'

'I suppose your father left things in a mess?'

She looked at me sharply. 'Father never went out of his library.'

She seemed to suppose that I knew more than I did. Looking round me, I found it hard to visualise a 'library'. I changed the subject.

'Aren't you going to find it rather a big house for one?'

It seemed a harmless, though uninspired, question. But Sally, instead of answering, simply sat staring before her. Although it was more as if she stared within her at some unpleasant thought.

I believe in acting upon impulse. 'Sally,' I said, 'I've got an idea. Why don't you sell this house, which *is* much too big for you, and come and live with me? We've plenty of room, and my father is the soul of generosity.'

She only shook her head. 'Thank you, Mel. No.' She still seemed absorbed by her own thoughts, disagreeable thoughts.

'You remember what you said the other day. About being glad I was living here. I'm likely to go on living here. I'd love to have you with me, Sally. Please think about it.'

She put down her ugly little teaplate on the ugly little table. She had taken a single small bite out of her pink cake. She stretched out her hand towards me; very tentatively, not nearly touching me. She gulped slightly. 'Mel . . .'

I moved to take her hand, but she drew it back. Suddenly she shook her head violently. Then she began to talk about her work.

She did not resume eating or drinking; and indeed both the cakes and the tea, which every now and then she pressed upon me in a casual way more like her former manner, were remarkably unappetising. But she talked interestingly and familiarly for about half an hour – about indifferent matters. Then she said, 'Forgive me, Mel. But I must be getting on.'

She rose. Of course I rose too. Then I hesitated.

'Sally . . . Please think about it. I'd like it so much. Please.'

'Thank you, Mel. I'll think about it.'

'Promise?'

'Promise . . . Thank you for coming to see me.'

'I want to see much more of you.'

She stood in the open front door. In the dusk she looked inexplicably harassed and woebegone.

'Come and see me whenever you want. Come to tea tomorrow and stay to dinner.' Anything to get her out of that horrible, horrible house.

But, as before, she only said, 'I'll think about it.'

Walking home it seemed to me that she could only have invited me out of obligation. I was much hurt; and much frightened by the change in her. As I reached my own gate it struck me that the biggest change of all was that she had never once smiled.

When five or six days later I had neither seen nor heard from Sally, I wrote asking her to visit me. For several days she did not reply at all: then she sent me another picture postcard, this time of some ancient bust in a museum, informing me that she would love to come when she had a little more time. I noticed that she had made a slight error in my address, which she had hastily and imperfectly corrected. The postman, of course, knew me. I could well imagine that there was much to do in Sally's house. Indeed, it was a house of the kind in which the work is never either satisfying or complete: an ever-open mouth of a house. But, despite the tales of her childhood, I could not imagine the Sally I knew doing it . . . I could not imagine what she was doing, and I admit that I did want to know.

Some time after that I came across Sally in the International Stores. It was not a shop I usually patronised, but Mr Orbit was out of my father's particular pickles. I could not help wondering whether Sally did not remember perfectly well that it was a shop in which I was seldom found.

She was there when I entered. She was wearing the same grimy slacks, and this time a white blouse which was worse than her former jumper, being plainly filthy. Against the autumn she wore a blue raincoat which I believed to be the same she had worn to school. She looked positively unkempt and far from well. She was nervously shovelling a little heap of dark blue bags and gaudy packets into a very ancient hold-all. Although the shop was fairly full, no one else was waiting to be served at the part of the counter where Sally stood. I walked up to her.

'Good morning, Sally.'

She clutched the ugly hold-all to her, as if I were about to snatch it. Then at once she became ostentatiously relaxed.

'Don't look at me like that,' she said. There was an upsetting little rasp in her voice. 'After all, Mel, you're not my mother.' Then she walked out of the shop.

'Your change, miss,' cried the International Stores shopman after her.

But she was gone. The other women in the shop watched her go as if she were the town tart. Then they closed up along the section of counter where she had been standing.

'Poor thing,' said the shopman unexpectedly. He was

young. The other women looked at him malevolently; and gave their orders with conscious briskness.

Then came Sally's accident.

By this time there could be no doubt that something was much wrong with her; but I had always been very nearly her only friend in the town, and her behaviour to me made it difficult for me to help. It was not that I lacked will or, I think, courage; but that I was unable to decide how to set about the task. I was still thinking about it when Sally was run over. I imagine that her trouble, whatever it was, had affected her ordinary judgment. Apparently she stepped right under a lorry in the High Street, having just visited the post office. I learned shortly afterwards that she refused to have letters delivered at her house, but insisted upon them being left poste restante.

When she had been taken to the Cottage Hospital, the matron, Miss Garvice, sent for me. Everyone knew that I was Sally's friend.

'Do you know who is her next-of-kin?'

'I doubt whether she has such a thing in this country.'

'Friends?'

'Only me that I know of.' I had always wondered about the mysterious informant of Dr Tessler's passing.

Miss Garvice considered for a moment.

'I'm worried about her house. Strictly speaking, in all the circumstances, I suppose I ought to tell the police, and ask them to keep an eye on it. But I am sure she would prefer me to ask you.'

From her tone I rather supposed that Miss Garvice knew nothing of the recent changes in Sally. Or perhaps she thought it best to ignore them.

'As you live so close, I wonder if it would be too much to ask you just to look in every now and then? Perhaps daily might be best?'

I think I accepted mainly because I suspected that something in Sally's life might need, for Sally's sake, to be kept from the wrong people.

'Here are her keys.'

It was a numerous assembly for such a commonplace establishment as Sally's.

'I'll do it as I say, Miss Garvice. But how long do you think it will be?'

'Hard to say. But I don't think Sally's going to die.'

One trouble was that I felt compelled to face the assignment unaided; because I knew no one in the town who seemed likely to regard Sally's predicament with the sensitiveness and delicacy – and indeed love – which I suspected were essential. There was also a dilemma about whether or not I should explore the house. Doubtless I had no right; but to do so might, on the other hand, possibly be regarded as in Sally's 'higher interests'. I must acknowledge, none the less, that my decision to proceed was considerably inspired by curiosity. This did not mean that I should involve others in whatever might be disclosed. Even that odious sitting-room would do Sally's reputation no good . . .

Miss Garvice had concluded by suggesting that I perhaps ought to pay my first visit at once. I went home to lunch. Then I set out.

Among the first things I discovered were that Sally kept every single door in the house locked: and that the remains of the tea I had taken with her weeks before still lingered in the sitting-room; not, mercifully, the food, but the plates, and cups, and genteel little knives, and the teapot with leaves and liquor at the bottom of it.

Giving on to the passage from the front door was a room adjoining the sitting-room, and corresponding to it at the back of the house. Presumably one of these rooms was intended by the builder (the house was not of a kind to have had an architect) for use as a dining-room, the other as a drawing-room. I went through the keys. They were big keys, the doors and locks being pretentiously over-sized. In the end the door opened. I noticed a stale cold smell. The room appeared to be in complete darkness. Possibly Dr Tessler's library?

I groped round the inside of the door-frame for an electric light switch, but could find nothing. I took an-other half-step inside. The room seemed blacker than ever; and the stale cold smell somewhat stronger. I de-cided to defer exploration until later.

I shut the door and went upstairs. The ground-floor rooms were high, which made the stairs many and steep.

On the first floor were two rooms; corresponding in plan to the two rooms below. It could be called neither an imaginative design, nor a convenient one. I tried the front room first, again going through the rigmarole with the keys. The room was in a dilapidated condition;

and contained nothing but a considerable mass of papers. They appeared once to have been stacked on the bare floor; but the stacks had long since fallen over, and their component elements accumulated a deep top-dressing of flaky black particles. The grime was of that ultimate kind which seems to have an actually greasy consistency: the idea of further investigating those neglected masses of scroll and manuscript made me shudder.

The back room was a bedroom, presumably Sally's. All the curtains were drawn, and I had to turn on the light. It contained what must truly be termed, in the worn phrase, 'a few sticks of furniture'; all in the same period as the pieces in the sitting-room, though more exiguous and spidery-looking. The inflated size and height of the room, the heavy plaster cornice and even heavier plaster rose in the centre of the cracked ceiling, emphasised the sparseness of the anachronistic furnishing. There was, however, a more modern double-divan bed, very low on the floor, and looking as if it had been slept in but not remade for weeks. Someone seemed to have arisen rather suddenly, as at an alarm-clock. I tried to pull open a drawer in the rickety dressing-table. It squeaked and stuck; and proved to contain some pathetic-looking underclothes of Sally's. The long curtains were very heavy and dark green.

It was a depressing investigation, but I persisted.

The second floor gave the appearance of having been originally one room, reached from a small landing. There was marked evidence of unskilled cuttings and bodgings; aimed, it was clear, at partitioning off this single vast room in order to form a bathroom and lavatory, and a passage giving access thereto. Could the house have been originally built without these necessary amenities? Anything seemed possible. I remembered the chestnut about the architect who forgot the staircase.

But there was something here which I found not only squalid but vaguely frightening. The original door, giving from the small landing into the one room, showed every sign of having been forcibly burst open; and from the inside (characteristically, it had been hung to open outwards). The damage was seemingly not recent (although it is not easy to date such a thing); but the shattered door still hung dejectedly outward from its weighty lower hinge only, and, in fact, made it almost impossible to enter the room at all. Gingerly I forced it a little more forward. The ripped woodwork of the heavy door shrieked piercingly as I dragged at it. I looked in. The room, such as it had ever been, had been finally wrecked by the introduction of the batten partition which separated it from the bathroom and was covered with blistered dark-brown varnish. The only contents were a few decaying toys. The nursery; as I remembered from the exterior prospect. Through the gap between the sloping door and its frame I looked at the barred windows. Like everything else in the house, the bars seemed very heavy. I looked again at the toys. I observed that *all* of them seemed to be woolly animals. They were rotted with moth and mould; but not so much so as to conceal the fact that at least some of them appeared also to have been mutilated. There were the decomposing leg of a teddy bear, inches away from the main torso; the severed head of a fanciful stuffed bird. It was as unpleasant a scene as every other in the house.

What had Sally been doing all day? As I had suspected, clearly not cleaning the house. There remained the kitchen quarters; and, of course, the late Doctor's library.

There were odd scraps of food about the basement, and signs of recent though sketchy cooking. I was almost surprised to discover that Sally had not lived on air. In general, however, the basement suggested nothing more unusual than the familiar feeling of wonder at the combined magnitude and cumbrousness of cooking operations in the homes of our middle-class great-grandfathers.

I looked round for a candle with which to illumine the library. I even opened various drawers, bins, and cupboards. It seemed that there were no candles. In any case, I thought, shivering slightly in the descending dusk, the library was probably a job for more than a single candle. Next time I would provide myself with my father's imposing flashlamp.

There seemed nothing more to be done. I had not even taken off my coat. I had discovered little which was calculated to solve the mystery. Could Sally be doping herself? It really seemed a theory. I turned off the kitchen light, ascended to the ground floor, and, shutting the front door, descended again to the garden. I eyed the collapsed front gate with new suspicion. Some time later I realised that I had re-locked none of the inside doors.

Next morning I called at the Cottage Hospital.

'In a way,' said Miss Garvice, 'she's much better. Quite surprisingly so.'

'Can I see her?'

'I'm afraid not. She's unfortunately had a very restless night.' Miss Garvice was sitting at her desk with a large yellow cat in her lap. As she spoke, the cat gazed up into her face with a look of complacent interrogation.

'Not pain?'

'Not exactly, I think.' Miss Garvice turned the cat's head downward towards her knee. She paused before saying: 'She's been weeping all night. And talking too. More hysterical than delirious. In the end we had to move her out of the big ward.'

'What does she say?'

'It wouldn't be fair to our patients if we repeated what they say when they're not themselves.'

'I suppose not. Still—'

'I admit that I cannot at all understand what's the matter with her. With her mind, I mean, of course.'

'She's suffering from shock.'

'Yes . . . But when I said "mind", I should perhaps have said "emotions".' The cat jumped from Miss Garvice's lap to the floor. It began to rub itself against my stockings. Miss Garvice followed it with her eyes. 'Were you able to get to her house?'

'I looked in for a few minutes.'

Miss Garvice wanted to question me; but she stopped herself and only asked, 'Everything in order?'

'As far as I could see.'

'I wonder if you would collect together a few things, and bring them when you next come. I am sure I can leave it to you.'

'I'll see what I can do.' Remembering the house, I wondered what I *could* do. I rose. 'I'll look in tomorrow, if I may.' The cat followed me to the door purring. 'Perhaps I shall be able to see Sally then.'

Miss Garvice only nodded.

The truth was that I could not rest until I had investigated that back room. I was afraid, of course; but much more curious. Even my fear, I felt, perhaps wrongly, was more fear of the unknown than of anything I imagined myself likely in fact to find. Had there been a sympathetic friend available, I should have been glad of his company (it was a job for a man, or for no one). As it was, loyalty to Sally sent me, as before, alone.

During the morning it had become more and more overcast. In the middle of lunch it began to rain. Throughout the afternoon it rained more and more heavily. My mother said I was mad to go out, but I donned a pair of heavy walking shoes and my riding mackintosh. I had borrowed my father's flashlamp before he left that morning for his business.

I first entered the sitting-room, where I took off my mackintosh and saturated beret. It would perhaps have been more sensible to hang the dripping objects in the lower regions; but I think I felt it was wise not to leave them too far from the front door. I stood for a time in front of the mirror combing my matted hair. The light was fading fast, and it was difficult to see very much. The gusty wind hurled the rain against the big bay window, down which it descended like a rippling membrane of wax, distorting what little prospect remained outside. The window frame leaked copiously, making little pools on the floor.

I pulled up the collar of my sweater, took the flash-lamp, and entered the back room. Almost at once in the beam of light, I found the switch. It was placed at the normal height, but about three feet from the doorway: as if the intention were precisely to make it impossible for the light to be switched on – or off – from the door. I turned it on.

I had speculated extensively, but the discovery still surprised me. Within the original walls had been laid three courses of stonework, which continued overhead to form an arched vault under the ceiling. The grey stones had been unskilfully laid, and the vault in particular looked likely to collapse. The inside of the door was reinforced with a single sheet of iron. There remained no window at all. A crude system of electric lighting had been installed, but there seemed provision for neither heating nor ventilation. Conceivably the room was intended for use in air-raids; it had palpably been in existence for some time. But in that case it was hard to see why it should still be inhabited as it so plainly was . . .

For within the dismal place were many rough wooden shelves laden with crumbling brown books; several battered wooden armchairs; a large desk covered with papers; and a camp bed, showing, like the bed upstairs, signs of recent occupancy. Most curious of all were a small ashtray by the bedside choked with cigarette ends, and an empty coffee cup. I lifted the pillow; underneath it were Sally's pyjamas, not folded, but stuffed away out of sight. It was difficult to resist the unpleasant idea that she had begun by sleeping in the room upstairs, but for some reason had moved down to this stagnant cavern; which, moreover, she had stated that her father had never left.

I like to think of myself as more imaginative than sensible. I had, for example, conceived it as possible that Dr Tessler had been stark raving mad, and that the room he never left would prove to be padded. But no room could be less padded than this one. It was much more like a prison. It seemed impossible that all through her childhood Sally's father had been under some kind of duress. The room also – and horribly – resembled a tomb. Could the Doctor have been one of those visionaries who are given to brooding upon The End, and to decking themselves with the symbols of mortality, like Donne with his shroud? It was difficult to believe in Sally emulating her father in this ... For some time, I think, I fought off the most probable solution, carefully giving weight to every other suggestion which my mind could muster up. In the end I faced the fact that more than an oubliette or a grave, the place resembled a fortress; and the suggestion that there was something in the house against which protection was necessary, was imperative. The locked doors, the scene of ruin on the second floor, Sally's behaviour. I had known it all the time.

I turned off the bleak light, hanging by its kinked flex. As I locked the library door, I wondered upon the unknown troubles which might have followed my failure of yesterday to leave the house as I had found it. I walked the few steps down the passage from the library to the sitting-room, at once preoccupied and alert. But, for my peace of mind, neither preoccupied nor alert enough. Because, although only for a moment, a second, a gleam, when in that almost-vanished light I re-entered the sitting-room, I saw him.

As if, for my benefit, to make the most of the little light, he stood right up in the big bay window. The view he presented to me was what I should call three-quarters back. But I could see a fraction of the outline of his face; entirely white (a thing which has to be seen to be believed) and with the skin drawn tight over the bones as by a tourniquet. There was a suggestion of wispy hair. I think he wore black; a garment, I thought, like a frock-coat. He stood stooped and shadowy, except for the glimpse of white face. Of course I could not see his eyes. Needless to say, he was gone almost as soon as I beheld him; but it would be inexact to say that he went quite immediately. I had a scintilla of time in which to blink. I thought at first that dead or alive, it was Dr Tessler; but immediately afterwards I thought not.

That evening I tried to take my father into my confidence. I had always considered him the kindest of men, but one from whom I had been carried far out to sea. Now I was interested, as often with people, by the unexpectedness of his response. After I had finished my story (although I did not tell him everything), to which he listened carefully, sometimes putting an intelligent question about a point I had failed to illuminate, he said, 'If you want my opinion, I'll give it to you.'

'Please.'

'It's simple enough. The whole affair is no business of yours.' He smiled to take the sting out of the words, but underneath he seemed unusually serious.

'I'm fond of Sally. Besides Miss Garvice asked me.'

'Miss Garvice asked you to look in and see if there was any post; not to poke and pry about the house.'

It was undoubtedly my weak point. But neither was it an altogether strong one for him. 'Sally wouldn't let the postman deliver,' I countered. 'She was collecting her letters from the post office at the time she was run over. I can't imagine why.'

'Don't try,' said my father.

'But,' I said, 'what I saw? Even if I *had* no right to go all over the house.'

'Mel,' said my father, 'you're supposed to write novels. Haven't you noticed by this time that everyone's lives are full of things you can't understand? The exceptional thing is the thing you *can* understand. I remember a man I knew when I was first in London . . .' He

27

broke off. 'But fortunately we don't *have* to understand. And for that reason we've no right to scrutinise other people's lives too closely.'

Completely baffled, I said nothing.

My father patted me on the shoulder. 'You can fancy you see things when the light's not very good, you know. Particularly an artistic girl like you, Mel.'

Even by my parent I still liked occasionally to be called a girl.

When I went up to bed it struck me that again something had been forgotten. This time it was Sally's 'few things'.

Naturally it was the first matter Miss Garvice mentioned.

'I'm very sorry. I forgot. I think it must have been the rain,' I continued, excusing myself like an adolescent to authority.

Miss Garvice very slightly clucked her tongue. But her mind was on something else. She went to the door of her room.

'Serena!'

'Yes, Miss Garvice?'

'See that I'm not disturbed for a few minutes, will you, please? I'll call you again.'

'Yes, Miss Garvice.' Serena disappeared, mousily shutting the door.

'I want to tell you something in confidence.'

I smiled. Confidences pre-announced are seldom worth while.

'You know our routine here. We've been making various tests on Sally. One of them roused our suspicion.' Miss Garvice scraped a Swan Vesta on the composition striker which stood on her desk. For the moment she had forgotten the relative cigarette. 'Did you know that Sally was pregnant?'

'No,' I replied. But it might provide an explanation. Of a few things.

'Normally, of course, I shouldn't tell you. Or anyone else. But Sally is in such a hysterical state. And you say you know of no relatives?'

'None. What can I do?'

'I wonder if you would consider having her to stay with you? Not at once, of course. When we discharge her. Sally's going to need a friend.'

'She won't come. Or she wouldn't. I've already pressed her.'

Miss Garvice now was puffing away like a traction engine. 'Why did you do that?'

'I'm afraid that's my business.'

'You don't know who the father is?'

I said nothing.

'It's not as if Sally were a young girl. To be perfectly frank, there are things about her condition which I don't like.'

It was my turn for a question.

'What about the accident? Hasn't that affected matters?'

'Strangely enough, no. Although it's nothing less than a miracle. Of one kind or the other,' said Miss Garvice, trying to look broad-minded.

I felt that we were unlikely to make further progress. Assuring Miss Garvice that in due course I should invite Sally once more, I asked again if I could see her.

'I am sorry. But it's out of the question for Sally to see anyone.'

I was glad that Miss Garvice did not revert to the subject of Sally's few things, although, despite everything, I felt guilty for having forgotten them. Particularly because I had no wish to go back for them. It was out of the question even to think of explaining my real reasons to Miss Garvice, and loyalty to Sally continued to weigh heavily with me; but something must be devised. Moreover I must not take any step which might lead to someone else being sent to Sally's house. The best I could think of was to assemble some of my own 'things' and say they were Sally's. It would be for Sally to accept the substitution.

But the question which struck me next morning was whether the contamination in Sally's house could be brought to an end by steps taken in the house itself; or whether it could have influence outside. Sally's mysterious restlessness, as reported by Miss Garvice, was far from reassuring; but on the whole I inclined to see it as an aftermath or revulsion. (Sally's pregnancy I refused at this point to consider at all.) It was impossible to doubt that immediate action of some kind was vital. Exorcism? Or, conceivably, arson? I doubt whether I am one to whom the former would ever strongly appeal: certainly not as a means of routing something so apparently sensible to feeling as to sight. The latter, on the other hand, might well be defeated (apart from other difficulties) by that stone strong-box of a library. Flight? I considered it long and seriously. But still it seemed that my strongest motive in the whole affair was pity for Sally. So I stayed.

I did not visit the hospital that morning, from complete perplexity as to what there to do or say; but instead, during the afternoon, wandered back to the house. Despite my horror of the place, I thought that I might hit upon something able to suggest a course of action. I would look more closely at those grimy papers; and even at the books in the library. The idea of burning the place down was still by no means out of my mind. I would further ponder the inflammability of the house, and the degree of risk to the neighbours ... All the time, of course, I was completely miscalculating my own strength and what was happening to me.

But as I hoisted the fallen gate, my nerve suddenly left me; again, something which had never happened to me before, either in the course of these events or at any previous time. I felt very sick. I was much afraid lest I faint. My body felt simultaneously tense and insubstantial.

Then I became aware that Mr Orbit's delivery boy was staring at me from the gate of the dentist's house opposite. I must have presented a queer spectacle because the boy seemed to be standing petrified. His mouth, I saw, was wide open. I knew the boy quite well. It was essential for all kinds of reasons that I conduct myself suitably. The boy stood, in fact, for public opinion. I took a couple of deep breaths, produced the weighty bunch of keys from my handbag, and ascended the steps as steadily as possible.

Inside the house, I made straight for the basement, with a view to a glass of water. With Mr Orbit's boy no longer gaping at me, I felt worse than ever; so that, even before I could look for a tumbler or reach the tap, I had to sink upon one of the two battered kitchen chairs. All my hair was damp, and my clothes felt unbearably heavy.

Then I became aware that steps were descending the basement staircase.

I completed my sequence of new experiences by fainting indeed.

I came round to the noise of an animal; a snuffling, grunting cry, which seemed to come, with much persistence, from the floor above. I seemed to listen to it for some time, even trying, though failing, to identify what animal it was; before recovering more fully, and realising that Sally was leaning back against the dresser and staring at me.

'Sally! It was you.'

'Who did you think it was? It's my house.'

She no longer wore the stained grey slacks, but was dressed in a very curious way, about which I do not think it fair to say more. In other ways also, the change in her had become complete: her eyes had a repulsive lifelessness; the bone structure of her face, previously so fine, had altered unbelievably. There was an unpleasant croak in her voice, precisely as if her larynx had lost flexibility.

'Will you please return my keys?'

I even had difficulty in understanding what she said; although doubtless my shaky condition did not help. Very foolishly, I rose to my feet, while Sally glared at me with her changed eyes. I had been lying on the stone floor. There was a bad pain in the back of my head and neck.

'Glad to see you're better, Sally. I didn't expect you'd be about for some time yet.' My words were incredibly foolish.

She said nothing, but only stretched out her hand. It too was changed: it had become grey and bony, with protruding knotted veins.

I handed her the big bunch of keys. I wondered how she had entered the house without them. The animal wailing above continued without intermission. To it now seemed to be added a noise which struck me as resembling that of a pig scrabbling. Involuntarily I glanced upwards to the ceiling.

Sally snatched the keys, snatched them gently and softly, not violently; then cast her unblinking eyes upwards in parody of mine, and emitted an almost deafening shriek of laughter.

'Do you love children, Mel? Would you like to see my baby?'

Truly it was the last straw; and I do not know quite how I behaved.

Now Sally seemed filled with terrible pride. 'Let me tell you, Mel,' she said, 'that it's possible for a child to be born in a manner you'd never dream of.'

I had begun to shudder again, but Sally clutched hold of me with her grey hand and began to drag me up the basement stairs.

'Will you be godmother? Come and see your god-child, Mel.'

The noise was coming from the library. I clung to the top of the basement baluster. Distraught as I was, I now realised that the scrabbling sound was connected with the tearing to pieces of Dr Tessler's books. But it was the wheezy, throaty cry of the creature which most turned my heart and sinews to water.

Or to steel. Because as Sally tugged at me, trying to pull me away from the baluster and into the library, I suddenly realised that she had no strength at all. Whatever else had happened to her, she was weak as a wraith.

I dragged myself free from her, let go of the baluster, and made toward the front door. Sally began to scratch my face and neck, but I made a quite capable job of defending myself. Sally then began to call out in her un-natural voice: she was trying to summon the creature into the passage. She scraped and tore at me, while panting out a stream of dreadful endearments to the thing in the library.

In the end, I found that my hands were about her throat, which was bare despite the cold weather. I could stand no more of that wrecked voice. Immediately she began to kick; and the shoes she was wearing seemed to have metal toes. I had the final awful fancy that she had acquired iron feet. Then I threw her from me on the floor of the passage, and fled from the house.

It was now dark; somehow darker outside the house than inside it; and I found that I still had strength enough to run all the way home.

I went away for a fortnight, although on general grounds it was the last thing I had wanted to do. At the end of that time, and with Christmas drawing near, I returned to my parents' house; I was not going to permit Sally to upset my plan for a present way of life.

At intervals through the winter I peered at Sally's house from the corner of the cul-de-sac in which it stood; but never saw a sign of occupancy or change.

I had learned from Miss Garvice that Sally had simply 'disappeared' from the Cottage Hospital.

'Disappeared?'

'Long before she was due for discharge, I need hardly say.'

'How did it happen?'

'The night nurse was going her rounds and noticed that the bed was empty.'

Miss Garvice was regarding me as if I were a material witness. Had we been in Miss Garvice's room at the hospital, Serena would have been asked to see that we were not disturbed.

Sally had not been back long enough to be much noticed in the town; and I observed that soon no one mentioned her at all.

Then, one day between Easter and Whitsun, I found she was at the front door.

'Hallo, Mel.'

Again she was taking up the conversation. She was as until last autumn she had always been; with that strange imperishable untended prettiness of hers, and her sweet absent smile. She wore a white dress.

'Sally!' What could one say?

Our eyes met. She saw that she would have to come straight to the point.

'I've sold my house.'

I kept my head. 'I said it was too big for you. Come in.'

She entered.

'I've bought a villa. In the Cyclades.'

'For your work?'

She nodded. 'The house fetched a price of course. And my father left me more than I expected.'

I said something banal.

Already she was lying on the big sofa, and looking at me over the arm. 'Mel, I should like you to come and stay with me. For a long time. As long as you can. You're a free agent, and you can't want to stay here.'

Psychologists, I recollected, have ascertained that the comparative inferiority of women in contexts described as purely intellectual is attributable to the greater discouragement and repression of their curiosity when children.

'Thank you, Sally. But I'm quite happy here, you know.'

'You're *not*. Are you, Mel?'
'No. I'm not.'
'Well then?'
One day I shall probably go.

Ringing the Changes

He had never been among those many who deeply dislike church bells, but the ringing that evening at Holihaven changed his view. Bells could certainly get on one's nerves he felt, although he had only just arrived in the town.

He had been too well aware of the perils attendant upon marrying a girl twenty-four years younger than himself to add to them by a conventional honeymoon. The strange force of Phrynne's love had borne both of them away from their previous selves: in him a formerly haphazard and easy-going approach to life had been replaced by much deep planning to wall in happiness; and she, though once thought cold and choosy, would now agree to anything as long as she was with him. He had said that if they were to marry in June, it would be at the cost of not being able to honeymoon until October. Had they been courting longer, he had explained, gravely smiling, special arrangements could have been made; but, as it was, business claimed him. This, indeed, was true; because his business position was less influential than he had led Phrynne to believe. Finally, it would have been impossible for them to have courted longer, because they had courted from the day they met, which was less than six weeks before the day they married.

'"A village",' he had quoted as they entered the branch-line train at the junction (itself sufficiently remote), '"from which (it was said) persons of sufficient longevity might hope to reach Liverpool Street."' By now he was able to make jokes about age, although perhaps he did so rather too often.

'Who said that?'

'Bertrand Russell.'

She had looked at him with her big eyes in her tiny face.

'Really.' He had smiled confirmation.

'I'm not arguing.' She had still been looking at him. The romantic gas light in the charming period compartment had left him uncertain whether she was smiling back or not. He had given himself the benefit of the doubt, and kissed her.

The guard had blown his whistle and they had rumbled out into the darkness. The branch line swung so sharply away from the main line that Phrynne had been almost toppled from her seat.

'Why do we go so slowly when it's so flat?'

'Because the engineer laid the line up and down the hills and valleys such as they are, instead of cutting through and embanking over them.' He liked being able to inform her.

'How do you know? Gerald! You said you hadn't been to Holihaven before.'

'It applies to most of the railways in East Anglia.'

39

'So that even though it's flatter, it's slower?'

'Time matters less.'

'I should have hated going to a place where time mattered or that you'd been to before. You'd have had nothing to remember me by.'

He hadn't been quite sure that her words exactly expressed her thoughts, but the thought had lightened his heart.

Holihaven station could hardly have been built in the days of the town's magnificence, for they were in the Middle Ages; but it still implied grander functions than came its way now. The platforms were long enough for visiting London expresses, which had since gone elsewhere; and the architecture of the waiting rooms would have been not insufficient for occasional use by foreign royalty. Oil lamps on perches like those occupied by macaws lighted the uniformed staff, who numbered two and, together with every native of Holihaven, looked like storm-habituated mariners.

The station-master and porter, as Gerald took them to be, watched him approach down the platform, with a heavy suitcase in each hand and Phrynne walking deliciously by his side. He saw one of them address a remark to the other, but neither offered to help. Gerald had to put down the cases in order to give up their tickets. The other passengers had already disappeared.

'Where's the Bell?'

Gerald had found the hotel in a reference book. It was the only one allotted to Holihaven. But as Gerald spoke, and before the ticket collector could answer, the sudden deep note of an actual bell rang through the darkness. Phrynne caught hold of Gerald's sleeve.

Ignoring Gerald, the station-master, if such he was, turned to his colleague. 'They're starting early.'

'Every reason to be in good time,' said the other man.

The station-master nodded, and put Gerald's tickets indifferently in his jacket pocket.

'Can you please tell me how I get to the Bell Hotel?'

The station-master's attention returned to him. 'Have you a room booked?'

'Certainly.'

'Tonight?' The station-master looked inappropriately suspicious.

'Of course.'

Again the station-master looked at the other man.

'It's them Pascoes.'

'Yes,' said Gerald. 'That's the name. Pascoe.'

'We don't use the Bell,' explained the station-master. 'But you'll find it in Wrack Street.' He gesticulated vaguely and unhelpfully. 'Straight ahead. Down Station Road. Then down Wrack Street. You can't miss it.'

'Thank you.'

As soon as they entered the town, the big bell began to boom regularly.

'What narrow streets!' said Phrynne.

'They follow the lines of the medieval city. Before the river silted up, Holihaven was one of the most important seaports in Great Britain.'

'Where's everybody got to?'

41

Although it was only six o'clock, the place certainly seemed deserted.

'Where's the hotel got to?' rejoined Gerald.

'Poor Gerald! Let me help.' She laid her hand beside his on the handle of the suitcase nearest to her, but as she was about fifteen inches shorter than he, she could be of little assistance. They must already have gone more than a quarter of a mile. 'Do you think we're in the right street?'

'Most unlikely, I should say. But there's no one to ask.'

'Must be early-closing day.'

The single deep notes of the bell were now coming more frequently.

'Why are they ringing that bell? Is it a funeral?'

'Bit late for a funeral.'

She looked at him a little anxiously.

'Anyway it's not cold.'

'Considering we're on the east coast it's quite astonishingly warm.'

'Not that I care.'

'I hope that bell isn't going to ring all night.'

She pulled on the suitcase. His arms were in any case almost parting from his body. 'Look! We've passed it.'

They stopped, and he looked back. 'How could we have done that?'

'Well, we have.'

She was right. He could see a big ornamental bell hanging from a bracket attached to a house about a hundred yards behind them.

They retraced their steps and entered the hotel. A

42

woman dressed in a navy-blue coat and skirt, with a good figure but dyed red hair and a face ridged with make-up, advanced upon them.

'Mr and Mrs Banstead? I'm Hilda Pascoe. Don, my husband, isn't very well.'

Gerald felt full of doubts. His arrangements were not going as they should. Never rely on guide-book recommendations. The trouble lay partly in Phrynne's insistence that they go somewhere he did not know. 'I'm sorry to hear that,' he said.

'You know what men are like when they're ill?' Mrs Pascoe spoke understandingly to Phrynne.

'Impossible,' said Phrynne. 'Or very difficult.'

'Talk about "Woman in our hours of ease".'

'Yes,' said Phrynne. 'What's the trouble?'

'It's always been the same trouble with Don,' said Mrs Pascoe; then checked herself. 'It's his stomach,' she said. 'Ever since he was a kid, Don's had trouble with the lining of his stomach.'

Gerald interrupted. 'I wonder if we could see our rooms?'

'So sorry,' said Mrs Pascoe. 'Will you register first?' She produced a battered volume bound in peeling imitation leather. 'Just the name and address.' She spoke as if Gerald might contribute a résumé of his life.

It was the first time he and Phrynne had ever registered in a hotel; but his confidence in the place was not increased by the long period which had passed since the registration above.

'We're always quiet in October,' remarked Mrs

43

Pascoe, her eyes upon him. Gerald noticed that her eyes were slightly bloodshot. 'Except sometimes for the bars, of course.'

'We wanted to come out of the season,' said Phrynne soothingly.

'Quite,' said Mrs Pascoe.

'Are we alone in the house?' enquired Gerald. After all the woman was probably doing her best.

'Except for Commandant Shotcroft. You won't mind him, will you? He's a regular.'

'I'm sure we shan't,' said Phrynne.

'People say the house wouldn't be the same without Commandant Shotcroft.'

'I see.'

'What's that bell?' asked Gerald. Apart from anything else, it really was much too near.

Mrs Pascoe looked away. He thought she looked shifty under her entrenched make-up. But she only said, 'Practice.'

'Do you mean there will be more of them later?'

She nodded. 'But never mind,' she said encouragingly. 'Let me show you to your room. Sorry there's no porter.'

Before they had reached the bedroom, the whole peal had commenced.

'Is this the quietest room you have?' enquired Gerald. 'What about the other side of the house?'

'This *is* the other side of the house. Saint Guthlac's is over there.' She pointed out through the bedroom door.

'Darling,' said Phrynne, her hand on Gerald's arm,

44

'they'll soon stop. They're only practising.'

Mrs Pascoe said nothing. Her expression indicated that she was one of those people whose friendliness has a precise and never-exceeded limit.

'If *you* don't mind,' said Gerald to Phrynne, hesitating.

'They have ways of their own in Holihaven,' said Mrs Pascoe. Her undertone of militancy implied, among other things, that if Gerald and Phrynne chose to leave, they were at liberty to do so. Gerald did not care for that either: her attitude would have been different, he felt, had there been anywhere else for them to go. The bells were making him touchy and irritable.

'It's a very pretty room,' said Phrynne. 'I adore four-posters.'

'Thank you,' said Gerald to Mrs Pascoe. 'What time's dinner?'

'Seven-thirty. You've time for a drink in the bar first.' She went.

'We certainly have,' said Gerald when the door was shut. 'It's only just six.'

'Actually,' said Phrynne, who was standing by the window looking down into the street, 'I *like* church bells.'

'All very well,' said Gerald, 'but on one's honeymoon they distract the attention.'

'Not mine,' said Phrynne simply. Then she added, 'There's still no one about.'

'I expect they're all in the bar.'

'I don't want a drink. I want to explore the town.'

'As you wish. But hadn't you better unpack?'

'I ought to, but I'm not going to. Not until after I've

seen the sea.' Such small shows of independence in her enchanted Gerald.

Mrs Pascoe was not about when they passed through the lounge, nor was there any sound of activity in the establishment.

Outside, the bells seemed to be booming and bounding immediately over their heads.

'It's like warriors fighting in the sky,' shouted Phrynne. 'Do you think the sea's down there?' She indicated the direction from which they had previously retraced their steps.

'I imagine so. The street seems to end in nothing. That would be the sea.'

'Come on. Let's run.' She was off, before he could even think about it. Then there was nothing to do but run after her. He hoped there were not eyes behind blinds.

She stopped, and held wide her arms to catch him. The top of her head hardly came up to his chin. He knew she was silently indicating that his failure to keep up with her was not a matter for self-consciousness.

'Isn't it beautiful?'

'The sea?' There was no moon; and little was discernible beyond the end of the street.

'Not only.'

'Everything but the sea. The sea's invisible.'

'You can smell it.'

'I certainly can't hear it.'

She slackened her embrace and cocked her head away from him.

'The bells echo so much, it's as if there were two churches.'

'I'm sure there are more than that. There always are in old towns like this.' Suddenly he was struck by the significance of his words in relation to what she had said. He shrank into himself, tautly listening.

'Yes,' cried Phrynne delightedly. 'It *is* another church.'

'Impossible,' said Gerald. 'Two churches wouldn't have practice ringing on the same night.'

'I'm quite sure. I can hear one lot of bells with my left ear, and another lot with my right.'

They had still seen no one. The sparse gas lights fell on the furnishings of a stone quay, small but plainly in regular use.

'The whole population must be ringing the bells.' His own remark discomfited Gerald.

'Good for them.' She took his hand. 'Let's go down on the beach and look for the sea.'

They descended a flight of stone steps at which the sea had sucked and bitten. The beach was as stony as the steps, but lumpier.

'We'll just go straight on,' said Phrynne. 'Until we find it.'

Left to himself, Gerald would have been less keen. The stones were very large and very slippery, and his eyes did not seem to be becoming accustomed to the dark.

'You're right, Phrynne, about the smell.'

'Honest sea smell.'

'Just as you say.' He took it rather to be the smell of

47

dense rotting weed; across which he supposed they must be slithering. It was not a smell he had previously encountered in such strength.

Energy could hardly be spared for thinking, and advancing hand in hand was impossible.

After various random remarks on both sides and the lapse of what seemed a very long time, Phrynne spoke again. 'Gerald, where is it? What sort of seaport is it that has no sea?'

She continued onwards, but Gerald stopped and looked back. He had thought the distance they had gone overlong, but was startled to see how great it was. The darkness was doubtless deceitful, but the few lights on the quay appeared as on a distant horizon.

The far glimmering specks still in his eyes, he turned and looked after Phrynne. He could barely see her. Perhaps she was progressing faster without him.

'Phrynne! Darling!'

Unexpectedly she gave a sharp cry.

'Phrynne!'

She did not answer.

'Phrynne!'

Then she spoke more or less calmly. 'Panic over. Sorry, darling. I stood on something.'

He realised that a panic it had indeed been; at least in him.

'You're all right?'

'Think so.'

He struggled up to her. 'The smell's worse than ever.' It was overpowering.

'I think it's coming from what I stepped on. My foot went right in, and then there was the smell.'

'I've never known anything like it.'

'Sorry darling,' she said gently mocking him. 'Let's go away.'

'Let's go back. Don't you think?'

'Yes,' said Phrynne. 'But I must warn you I'm very disappointed. I think that seaside attractions should include the sea.'

He noticed that as they retreated, she was scraping the sides of one shoe against the stones, as if trying to clean it.

'I think the whole place is a disappointment,' he said. 'I really must apologise. We'll go somewhere else.'

'I like the bells,' she replied, making a careful reservation.

Gerald said nothing.

'I don't want to go somewhere where you've been before.'

The bells rang out over the desolate unattractive beach. Now the sound seemed to be coming from every point along the shore.

'I suppose all the churches practise on the same night in order to get it over with,' said Gerald.

'They do it in order to see which can ring the loudest,' said Phrynne.

'Take care you don't twist your ankle.'

The din as they reached the rough little quay was such as to suggest that Phrynne's idea was literally true.

*

The Coffee Room was so low that Gerald had to dip beneath a sequence of thick beams.

'Why "Coffee Room"?' asked Phrynne, looking at the words on the door. 'I saw a notice that coffee will only be served in the lounge.'

'It's the *lucus a non lucendo* principle.'

'That explains everything. I wonder where we sit.' A single electric lantern, mass-produced in an antique pattern, had been turned on. The bulb was of that limited wattage which is peculiar to hotels. It did little to penetrate the shadows.

'The *lucus a non lucendo* principle is the principle of calling white black.'

'Not at all,' said a voice from the darkness. 'On the contrary. The word "black" comes from an ancient root which means "to bleach".'

They had thought themselves alone, but now saw a small man seated by himself at an unlighted corner table. In the darkness he looked like a monkey.

'I stand corrected,' said Gerald.

They sat at the table under the lantern.

The man in the corner spoke again. 'Why are you here at all?'

Phrynne looked frightened, but Gerald replied quietly. 'We're on holiday. We prefer it out of the season. I presume you are Commandant Shotcroft?'

'No need to presume.' Unexpectedly the Commandant switched on the antique lantern which was nearest to him. His table was littered with a finished meal. It struck Gerald that he must have switched off the light when he heard them approach the Coffee Room. 'I'm going anyway.'

'Are we late?' asked Phrynne, always the assuager of situations.

'No, you're not late,' called the Commandant in a deep moody voice. 'My meals are prepared half an hour before the time the rest come in. I don't like eating in company.' He had risen to his feet. 'So perhaps you'll excuse me.'

Without troubling about an answer, he stepped quickly out of the Coffee Room. He had cropped white hair; tragic, heavy-lidded eyes; and a round face which was yellow and lined.

A second later his head reappeared round the door.

'Ring,' he said; and again withdrew.

'Too many other people ringing,' said Gerald. 'But I don't see what else we can do.'

The Coffee Room bell, however, made a noise like a fire alarm.

Mrs Pascoe appeared. She looked considerably the worse for drink.

'Didn't see you in the bar.'

'Must have missed us in the crowd,' said Gerald amiably.

'Crowd?' enquired Mrs Pascoe drunkenly. Then, after a difficult pause, she offered them a hand-written menu.

They ordered; and Mrs Pascoe served them throughout. Gerald was apprehensive lest her indisposition increase during the course of the meal; but her insobriety, like her affability, seemed to have an exact and definite limit.

'All things considered, the food might be worse,' remarked Gerald, towards the end. It was a relief that something was going reasonably well. 'Not much of it, but at least the dishes are hot.'

When Phrynne translated this into a compliment to the cook, Mrs Pascoe said, 'I cooked it all myself, although I shouldn't be the one to say so.'

Gerald felt really surprised that she was in a condition to have accomplished this. Possibly, he reflected with alarm, she had had much practice under similar conditions.

'Coffee is served in the lounge,' said Mrs Pascoe.

They withdrew. In a corner of the lounge was a screen decorated with winning Elizabethan ladies in ruffs and hoops. From behind it projected a pair of small black boots. Phrynne nudged Gerald and pointed to them. Gerald nodded. They felt themselves constrained to talk about things which bored them.

The hotel was old and its walls thick. In the empty lounge the noise of the bells would not prevent conversation being overheard, but still came from all around, as if the hotel were a fortress beleaguered by surrounding artillery.

After their second cups of coffee, Gerald suddenly said he couldn't stand it.

'Darling, it's not doing us any harm. I think it's rather cosy.' Phrynne subsided in the wooden chair with its sloping back and long mud-coloured mock-velvet cushions; and opened her pretty legs to the fire.

'Every church in the town must be ringing its bells. It's been going on for two and a half hours and they never seem to take the usual breathers.'

'We wouldn't hear. Because of all the other bells ringing. I think it's nice of them to ring the bells for us.'

Nothing further was said for several minutes. Gerald was beginning to realise that they had yet to evolve a holiday routine.

'I'll get you a drink. What shall it be?'

'Anything you like. Whatever *you* have.' Phrynne was immersed in female enjoyment of the fire's radiance on her body.

Gerald missed this, and said 'I don't quite see why they have to keep the place like a hothouse. When I come back, we'll sit somewhere else.'

'Men wear too many clothes, darling,' said Phrynne drowsily.

Contrary to his assumption, Gerald found the lounge bar as empty as everywhere else in the hotel and the town. There was not even a person to dispense.

Somewhat irritably Gerald struck a brass bell which stood on the counter. It rang out sharply as a pistol shot.

Mrs Pascoe appeared at a door among the shelves. She had taken off her jacket, and her make-up had begun to run.

'A cognac, please. Double. And a Kummel.'

Mrs Pascoe's hands were shaking so much that she could not get the cork out of the brandy bottle.

'Allow me.' Gerald stretched his arm across the bar.

53

Mrs Pascoe stared at him blearily. 'Okay. But I must pour it.'

Gerald extracted the cork and returned the bottle. Mrs Pascoe slopped a far from precise dose into a balloon.

Catastrophe followed. Unable to return the bottle to the high shelf where it resided, Mrs Pascoe placed it on a waist-level ledge. Reaching for the alembic of Kummel, she swept the three-quarters-full brandy bottle on to the tiled floor. The stuffy air became fogged with the fumes of brandy from behind the bar.

At the door from which Mrs Pascoe had emerged appeared a man from the inner room. Though still youngish, he was puce and puffy, and in his braces, with no collar. Streaks of sandy hair laced his vast red scalp. Liquor oozed all over him, as if from a perished gourd. Gerald took it that this was Don.

The man was too drunk to articulate. He stood in the doorway, clinging with each red hand to the ledge, and savagely struggling to flay his wife with imprecations.

'How much?' said Gerald to Mrs Pascoe. It seemed useless to try for the Kummel. The hotel must have another bar.

'Three and six,' said Mrs Pascoe, quite lucidly; but Gerald saw that she was about to weep.

He had the exact sum. She turned her back on him and flicked the cash register. As she returned from it, he heard the fragmentation of glass as she stepped on a piece of the broken bottle. Gerald looked at her husband out of the corner of his eye. The sagging, loose-mouthed figure made him shudder. Something moved him.

'I'm sorry about the accident,' he said to Mrs Pascoe. He held the balloon in one hand, and was just going.

Mrs Pascoe looked at him. The slow tears of desperation were edging down her face, but she now seemed quite sober. 'Mr Banstead,' she said in a flat, hurried voice. 'May I come and sit with you and your wife in the lounge? Just for a few minutes.'

'Of course.' It was certainly not what he wanted, and he wondered what would become of the bar, but he felt unexpectedly sorry for her, and it was impossible to say no.

To reach the flap of the bar, she had to pass her husband. Gerald saw her hesitate for a second; then she advanced resolutely and steadily, and looking straight before her. If the man had let go with his hands, he would have fallen; but as she passed him, he released a great gob of spit. He was far too incapable to aim, and it fell on the side of his own trousers. Gerald lifted the flap for Mrs Pascoe and stood back to let her precede him from the bar. As he followed her, he heard her husband maundering off into unintelligible inward searchings.

'The Kummel!' said Mrs Pascoe, remembering in the doorway.

'Never mind,' said Gerald. 'Perhaps I could try one of the other bars?'

'Not tonight. They're shut. I'd better go back.'

'No. We'll think of something else.' It was not yet nine o'clock, and Gerald wondered about the licensing justices.

But in the lounge was another unexpected scene. Mrs Pascoe stopped as soon as they entered, and Gerald, caught between two imitation-leather armchairs, looked over her shoulder.

Phrynne had fallen asleep. Her head was slightly on one side, but her mouth was shut, and her body no more than gracefully relaxed, so that she looked most beautiful, and, Gerald thought, a trifle unearthly, like a dead girl in an early picture by Millais.

The quality of her beauty seemed also to have impressed Commandant Shotcroft; for he was standing silently behind her and looking down at her, his sad face transfigured. Gerald noticed that a leaf of the pseudo-Elizabethan screen had been folded back, revealing a small cretonne-covered chair, with an open tome face downward in its seat.

'Won't you join us?' said Gerald boldly. There was that in the Commandant's face which boded no hurt. 'Can I get you a drink?'

The Commandant did not turn his head, and for a moment seemed unable to speak. Then in a low voice he said, 'For a moment only.'

'Good,' said Gerald. 'Sit down. And you, Mrs Pascoe.' Mrs Pascoe was dabbing at her face. Gerald addressed the Commandant. 'What shall it be?'

'Nothing to drink,' said the Commandant in the same low mutter. It occurred to Gerald that if Phrynne awoke, the Commandant would go.

'What about you?' Gerald looked at Mrs Pascoe, earnestly hoping she would decline.

'No thanks.' She was glancing at the Commandant. Clearly she had not expected him to be there.

Phrynne being asleep, Gerald sat down too. He sipped his brandy. It was impossible to romanticise the action with a toast.

The events in the bar had made him forget about the bells. Now, as they sat silently round the sleeping Phrynne, the tide of sound swept over him once more.

'You mustn't think,' said Mrs Pascoe, 'that he's always like that.' They all spoke in hushed voices. All of them seemed to have reason to do so. The Commandant was again gazing sombrely at Phrynne's beauty.

'Of course not.' But it was hard to believe.

'The licensed business puts temptations in a man's way.'

'It must be very difficult.'

'We ought never to have come here. We were happy in South Norwood.'

'You must do good business during the season.'

'Two months,' said Mrs Pascoe bitterly, but still softly. 'Two and a half at the very most. The people who come during the season have no idea what goes on out of it.'

'What made you leave South Norwood?'

'Don's stomach. The doctor said the air would do him good.'

'Speaking of that, doesn't the sea go too far out? We went down on the beach before dinner, but couldn't see it anywhere.'

On the other side of the fire, the Commandant turned his eyes from Phrynne and looked at Gerald.

'I wouldn't know,' said Mrs Pascoe. 'I never have time to look from one year's end to the other.' It was a customary enough answer, but Gerald felt that it did not disclose the whole truth. He noticed that Mrs Pascoe glanced uneasily at the Commandant, who by now was staring neither at Phrynne nor at Gerald but at the toppling citadels in the fire.

'And now I must get on with my work,' continued Mrs Pascoe, 'I only came in for a minute.' She looked Gerald in the face. 'Thank you,' she said, and rose.

'Please stay a little longer,' said Gerald, 'Wait till my wife wakes up.' As he spoke, Phrynne slightly shifted.

'Can't be done,' said Mrs Pascoe, her lips smiling. Gerald noticed that all the time she was watching the Commandant from under her lids, and knew that were he not there, she would have stayed.

As it was, she went. 'I'll probably see you later to say goodnight. Sorry the water's not very hot. It's having no porter.'

The bells showed no sign of flagging.

When Mrs Pascoe had closed the door, the Commandant spoke.

'He was a fine man once. Don't think otherwise.'

'You mean Pascoe?'

The Commandant nodded seriously.

'Not my type,' said Gerald.

'DSO and bar. DFC and bar.'

'And now bar only. Why?'

'You heard what she said. It was a lie. They didn't leave South Norwood for the sea air.'

'So I supposed.'

'He got into trouble. He was fixed. He wasn't the kind of man to know about human nature and all its rottenness.'

'A pity,' said Gerald. 'But perhaps, even so, this isn't the best place for him?'

'It's the worst,' said the Commandant, a dark flame in his eyes. 'For him or anyone else.'

Again Phrynne shifted in her sleep: this time more convulsively, so that she nearly woke. For some reason the two men remained speechless and motionless until she was again breathing steadily. Against the silence within, the bells sounded louder than ever. It was as if the tumult were tearing holes in the roof.

'It's certainly a very noisy place,' said Gerald, still in an undertone.

'Why did you have to come tonight of all nights?' The Commandant spoke in the same undertone, but his vehemence was extreme.

'This doesn't happen often?'

'Once every year.'

'They should have told us.'

'They don't usually accept bookings. They've no right to accept them. When Pascoe was in charge they never did.'

'I expect that Mrs Pascoe felt they were in no position to turn away business.'

'It's not a matter that should be left to a woman.'

'Not much alternative surely?'

'At heart, women are creatures of darkness all the

time.' The Commandant's seriousness and bitterness left Gerald without a reply.

'My wife doesn't mind the bells,' he said after a moment. 'In fact she rather likes them.' The Commandant really was converting a nuisance, though an acute one, into a melodrama.

The Commandant turned and gazed at him. It struck Gerald that what he had just said in some way, for the Commandant, placed Phrynne also in a category of the lost.

'Take her away, man,' said the Commandant, with scornful ferocity.

'In a day or two perhaps,' said Gerald, patiently polite. 'I admit that we are disappointed with Holihaven.'

'Now. While there's still time. This *instant*.'

There was an intensity of conviction about the Commandant which was alarming.

Gerald considered. Even the empty lounge, with its dreary decorations and commonplace furniture, seemed inimical. 'They can hardly go on practising all night,' he said. But now it was fear that hushed his voice.

'Practising!' The Commandant's scorn flickered coldly through the overheated room.

'What else?'

'They're ringing to wake the dead.'

A tremor of wind in the flue momentarily drew on the already roaring fire. Gerald had turned very pale.

'That's a figure of speech,' he said, hardly to be heard.

'Not in Holihaven.' The Commandant's gaze had returned to the fire.

Gerald looked at Phrynne. She was breathing less heavily. His voice dropped to a whisper. 'What happens?'

The Commandant also was nearly whispering. 'No one can tell how long they have to go on ringing. It varies from year to year. I don't know why. You should be all right up to midnight. Probably for some while after. In the end the dead awake. First one or two, then all of them. Tonight even the sea draws back. You have seen that for yourself. In a place like this there are always several drowned each year. This year there've been more than several. But even so that's only a few. Most of them come not from the water but from the earth. It is not a pretty sight.'

'Where do they go?'

'I've never followed them to see. I'm not stark staring mad.' The red of the fire reflected in the Commandant's eyes. There was a long pause.

'I don't believe in the resurrection of the body,' said Gerald. As the hour grew later, the bells grew louder. 'Not of the body.'

'What other kind of resurrection is possible? Everything else is only theory. You can't even imagine it. No one can.'

Gerald had not argued such a thing for twenty years. 'So,' he said, 'you advise me to go. Where?'

'Where doesn't matter.'

'I have no car.'

'Then you'd better walk.'

'With her?' He indicated Phrynne only with his eyes.

'She's young and strong.' A forlorn tenderness lay within the Commandant's words. 'She's twenty years younger than you and therefore twenty years more important.'

'Yes,' said Gerald. 'I agree . . . What about you? What will you do?'

'I've lived here some time now. I know what to do.'

'And the Pascoes?'

'He's drunk. There is nothing in the world to fear if you're thoroughly drunk. DSO and bar. DFC and bar.'

'But you're not drinking yourself?'

'Not since I came to Holihaven. I lost the knack.'

Suddenly Phrynne sat up. 'Hallo,' she said to the Commandant; not yet fully awake. Then she said, 'What fun! The bells are still ringing.'

The Commandant rose, his eyes averted. 'I don't think there's anything more to say,' he remarked, addressing Gerald. 'You've still got time.' He nodded slightly to Phrynne, and walked out of the lounge.

'What have you still got time for?' asked Phrynne, stretching. 'Was he trying to convert you? I'm sure he's an Anabaptist.'

'Something like that,' said Gerald, trying to think.

'Shall we go to bed? Sorry, I'm so sleepy.'

'Nothing to be sorry about.'

'Or shall we go for another walk? That would wake me up. Besides, the tide might have come in.'

Gerald, although he half despised himself for it, found it impossible to explain to her that they should leave at once; without transport or a destination; walk all night if necessary. He said to himself that probably he would not go even were he alone.

'If you're sleepy, it's probably a *good* thing.'

'Darling!'

'I mean with these bells. God knows when they will stop.' Instantly he felt a new pang of fear at what he had said.

Mrs Pascoe had appeared at the door leading to the bar, and opposite to that from which the Commandant had departed. She bore two steaming glasses on a tray. She looked about, possibly to confirm that the Commandant had really gone.

'I thought you might both like a nightcap. Ovaltine, with something in it.'

'Thank you,' said Phrynne. 'I can't think of anything nicer.'

Gerald set the glasses on a wicker table, and quickly finished his cognac.

Mrs Pascoe began to move chairs and slap cushions. She looked very haggard.

'Is the Commandant an Anabaptist?' asked Phrynne over her shoulder. She was proud of her ability to out-distance Gerald in beginning to consume a hot drink.

Mrs Pascoe stopped slapping for a moment. 'I don't know what that is,' she said.

'He's left his book,' said Phrynne, on a new tack.

'I wonder what he's reading,' continued Phrynne. 'Foxe's *Lives of the Martyrs*, I expect.' A small unusual devil seemed to have entered into her.

But Mrs Pascoe knew the answer. 'It's always the

same,' she said contemptuously. 'He only reads one. It's called *Fifteen Decisive Battles of the World*. He's been reading it ever since he came here. When he gets to the end, he starts again.'

'Should I take it up to him?' asked Gerald. It was neither courtesy nor inclination, but rather a fear lest the Commandant return to the lounge: a desire, after those few minutes of reflection, to cross-examine.

'Thanks very much,' said Mrs Pascoe, as if relieved of a similar apprehension. 'Room One. Next to the suit of Japanese armour.' She went on tipping and banging. To Gerald's inflamed nerves, her behaviour seemed too consciously normal.

He collected the book and made his way upstairs. The volume was bound in real leather, and the top of its pages were gilded: apparently a presentation copy. Outside the lounge, Gerald looked at the fly-leaf: in a very large hand was written 'To my dear Son, Raglan, on his being honoured by the Queen. From his proud Father, B. Shotcroft, Major-General.' Beneath the inscription a very ugly military crest had been appended by a stamper of primitive type.

The suit of Japanese armour lurked in a dark corner as the Commandant himself had done when Gerald had first encountered him. The wide brim of the helmet concealed the black eyeholes in the headpiece; the moustache bristled realistically. It was exactly as if the figure stood guard over the door behind it. On this door was no number, but, there being no other in sight, Gerald took it to be the door of Number One. A short way down the dim, empty passage was a window, the ancient sashes of which shook in the din and blast of the bells. Gerald knocked sharply.

If there was a reply, the bells drowned it; and he knocked again. When to the third knocking there was still no answer, he gently opened the door. He really had to know whether all would or could be well if Phrynne, and doubtless he also, were at all costs to remain in their room until it was dawn. He looked into the room and caught his breath.

There was no artificial light, but the curtains, if there were any, had been drawn back from the single window, and the bottom sash forced up as far as it would go. On the floor by the dusky void, a maelstrom of sound, knelt the Commandant, his cropped white hair faintly catching the moonless glimmer, as his head lay on the sill, like that of a man about to be guillotined. His face was in his hands, but slightly sideways, so that Gerald received a shadowy distorted idea of his expression. Some might have called it ecstatic, but Gerald found it agonised. It frightened him more than anything which had yet happened. Inside the room the bells were like plunging, roaring lions.

He stood for some considerable time quite unable to move. He could not determine whether or not the Commandant knew he was there. The Commandant gave no direct sign of it, but more than once he writhed and shuddered in Gerald's direction, like an unquiet sleeper made more unquiet by an interloper. It was a matter of doubt whether Gerald should leave the book;

and he decided to do so mainly because the thought of further contact with it displeased him. He crept into the room and softly laid it on a hardly visible wooden trunk at the foot of the plain metal bedstead. There seemed no other furniture in the room. Outside the door, the hanging mailed fingers of the Japanese figure touched his wrist.

He had not been away from the lounge for long, but it was long enough for Mrs Pascoe to have begun to drink again. She had left the tidying up half-completed, or rather the room half-disarranged; and was leaning against the overmantel, drawing heavily on a dark tumbler of whisky. Phrynne had not yet finished her Ovaltine.

'How long before the bells stop?' asked Gerald as soon as he opened the lounge door. Now he was resolved that, come what might, they must go. The impossibility of sleep should serve as an excuse.

'I don't expect Mrs Pascoe can know any more than we can,' said Phrynne.

'You should have told us about this – this annual event before accepting our booking.'

Mrs Pascoe drank some more whisky. Gerald suspected that it was neat. 'It's not always the same night,' she said throatily, looking at the floor.

'We're not staying,' said Gerald wildly.

'Darling!' Phrynne caught him by the arm.

'Leave this to me, Phrynne.' He addressed Mrs Pascoe. 'We'll pay for the room, of course. Please order me a car.'

Mrs Pascoe was now regarding him stonily. When he asked for a car, she gave a very short laugh. Then her face changed, she made an effort, and she said, 'You mustn't take the Commandant so seriously, you know.'

Phrynne glanced quickly at her husband.

The whisky was finished. Mrs Pascoe placed the empty glass on the plastic overmantel with too much of a thud. 'No one takes Commandant Shotcroft seriously,' she said. 'Not even his nearest and dearest.'

'Has he any?' asked Phrynne. 'He seemed so lonely and pathetic.'

'He's Don and I's mascot,' she said, the drink interfering with her grammar. But not even the drink could leave any doubt about her rancour.

'I thought he had personality,' said Phrynne.

'That and a lot more, no doubt,' said Mrs Pascoe. 'But they pushed him out, all the same.'

'Out of what?'

'Cashiered, court-martialled, badges of rank stripped off, sword broken in half, muffled drums, the works.'

'Poor old man. I'm sure it was a miscarriage of justice.'

'That's because you don't know him.'

Mrs Pascoe looked as if she were waiting for Gerald to offer her another whisky.

'It's a thing he could never live down,' said Phrynne, brooding to herself, and tucking her legs beneath her. 'No wonder he's so queer if all the time it was a mistake.'

'I just told you it was not a mistake,' said Mrs Pascoe insolently.

'How can we possibly know?'

'*You* can't. *I* can. No one better.' She was at once aggressive and tearful.

'If you want to be paid,' cried Gerald, forcing himself in, 'make out your bill. Phrynne, come upstairs and pack.' If only he hadn't made her unpack between their walk and dinner.

Slowly Phrynne uncoiled and rose to her feet. She had no intention of either packing or departing, but nor was she going to argue. 'I shall need your help,' she said, softly. 'If I'm going to pack.'

In Mrs Pascoe there was another change. Now she looked terrified. 'Don't go. Please don't go. Not now. It's too late.'

Gerald confronted her. 'Too late for what?' he asked harshly.

Mrs Pascoe looked paler than ever. 'You said you wanted a car,' she faltered. 'You're too late.' Her voice trailed away.

Gerald took Phrynne by the arm. 'Come on up.'

Before they reached the door, Mrs Pascoe made a further attempt. 'You'll be all right if you stay. Really you will.' Her voice, normally somewhat strident, was so feeble that the bells obliterated it. Gerald observed that from somewhere she had produced the whisky bottle and was refilling her tumbler.

With Phrynne on his arm he went first to the stout front door. To his surprise it was neither locked nor bolted, but opened at a half-turn of the handle. Outside the building the whole sky was full of bells, the air an inferno of ringing.

He thought that for the first time Phrynne's face also seemed strained and crestfallen. 'They've been ringing too long,' she said, drawing close to him. 'I wish they'd stop.'

'We're packing and going. I needed to know whether we could get out this way. We must shut the door quietly.'

It creaked a bit on its hinges, and he hesitated with it half-shut, uncertain whether to rush the creak or to ease it. Suddenly, something dark and shapeless, with its arm seeming to hold a black vesture over its head, flitted, all sharp angles, like a bat, down the narrow ill-lighted street, the sound of its passage audible to none. It was the first being that either of them had seen in the streets of Holihaven; and Gerald was acutely relieved that he alone had set eyes upon it. With his hand trembling, he shut the door much too sharply.

But no one could possibly have heard, although he stopped for a second outside the lounge. He could hear Mrs Pascoe now weeping hysterically; and again was glad that Phrynne was a step or two ahead of him. Upstairs the Commandant's door lay straight before them: they had to pass close beside the Japanese figure, in order to take the passage to the left of it.

But soon they were in their room, with the key turned in the big rim lock.

'Oh God,' cried Gerald, sinking on the double bed. 'It's pandemonium.' Not for the first time that evening he was instantly more frightened than ever by the unintended appositeness of his own words.

'It's pandemonium all right,' said Phrynne, almost calmly. 'And we're not going out in it.'

He was at a loss to divine how much she knew, guessed, or imagined; and any word of enlightenment from him might be inconceivably dangerous. But he was conscious of the strength of her resistance, and lacked the reserves to battle with it.

She was looking out of the window into the main street. 'We might *will* them to stop,' she suggested wearily.

Gerald was now far less frightened of the bells continuing than of their ceasing. But that they should go on ringing until day broke seemed hopelessly impossible.

Then one peel stopped. There could be no other explanation for the obvious diminuition in sound.

'You see!' said Phrynne.

Gerald sat up straight on the side of the bed.

Almost at once further sections of sound subsided, quickly one after the other, until only a single peal was left, that which had begun the ringing. Then the single peal tapered off into a single bell. The single bell tolled on its own, disjointedly, five or six or seven times. Then it stopped, and there was nothing.

Gerald's head was a cave of echoes, mountingly muffled by the noisy current of his blood.

'Oh goodness,' said Phrynne, turning from the window and stretching her arms above her head. 'Let's go somewhere else tomorrow.' She began to take off her dress.

Sooner than usual they were in bed, and in one another's arms. Gerald had carefully not looked out of the
window, and neither of them suggested that it should be
opened, as they usually did.

'As it's a four-poster, shouldn't we draw the curtains?'
asked Phrynne. 'And be really snug? After those damned
bells?'

'We should suffocate.'

'They only drew the curtains when people were likely
to pass through the room.'

'Darling, you're shivering. I think we *should* draw
them.'

'Lie still instead, and love me.'

But all his nerves were straining out into the silence.
There was no sound of any kind, beyond the hotel or
within it; not a creaking floorboard or a prowling cat or
a distant owl. He had been afraid to look at his watch
when the bells stopped, or since: the number of the dark
hours before they could leave Holihaven weighed on
him. The vision of the Commandant kneeling in the
dark window was clear before his eyes, as if the inter-
vening panelled walls were made of stage gauze; and the
thing he had seen in the street darted on its angular way
back and forth through memory.

Then passion began to open its petals within him,
layer upon slow layer; like an illusionist's red flower
which, without soil or sun or sap, grows as it is watched.
The languor of tenderness began to fill the musty room
with its texture and perfume. The transparent walls became again opaque, the old man's vaticinations mere

obsession. The street must have been empty, as it was now; the eye deceived.

But perhaps rather it was the boundless sequacity of love that deceived, and most of all in the matter of the time which had passed since the bells stopped ringing; for suddenly Phrynne drew very close to him, and he heard steps in the thoroughfare outside, and a voice calling. These were loud steps, audible from afar even through the shut window; and the voice had the possessed stridency of the street evangelist.

'The dead are awake!'

Not even the thick bucolic accent, the guttural vibrato of emotion, could twist or mask the meaning. At first Gerald lay listening with all his body, and concentrating the more as the noise grew; then he sprang from the bed and ran to the window.

A burly, long-limbed man in a seaman's jersey was running down the street, coming clearly into view for a second at each lamp, and between them lapsing into a swaying lumpy wraith. As he shouted his joyous message, he crossed from side to side and waved his arms like a negro. By flashes, Gerald could see that his weatherworn face was transfigured.

'The dead are awake!'

Already, behind him, people were coming out of their houses, and descending from the rooms above shops. There were men, women, and children. Most of them were fully dressed, and must have been waiting in silence and darkness for the call; but a few were dishevelled in night attire or the first garments which had come to hand. Some formed themselves into groups, and advanced arm in arm, as if towards the conclusion of a Blackpool beano. More came singly, ecstatic and waving their arms above their heads, as the first man had done. All cried out, again and again, with no cohesion or harmony. 'The dead are awake! The dead are awake!'

Gerald became aware that Phrynne was standing behind him.

'The Commandant warned me,' he said brokenly. 'We should have gone.'

Phrynne shook her head and took his arm. 'Nowhere to go,' she said. But her voice was soft with fear, and her eyes blank. 'I don't expect they'll trouble *us*.'

Swiftly Gerald drew the thick plush curtains, leaving them in complete darkness. 'We'll sit it out,' he said, slightly histrionic in his fear. 'No matter what happens.'

He scrambled across to the switch. But when he pressed it, light did not come. 'The current's gone. We must get back into bed.'

'Gerald! Come and help me.' He remembered that she was curiously vulnerable in the dark. He found his way to her, and guided her to the bed.

'No more love,' she said ruefully and affectionately, her teeth chattering.

He kissed her lips with what gentleness the total night made possible.

'They were going towards the sea,' she said timidly.

'We must think of something else.'

But the noise was still growing. The whole community seemed to be passing down the street, yelling the same dreadful words again and again.

'Do you think we can?'

'Yes,' said Gerald. 'It's only until tomorrow.'

'They can't be actually dangerous,' said Phrynne. 'Or it would be stopped.'

'Yes, of course.'

By now, as always happens, the crowd had amalgamated their utterances and were beginning to shout in unison. They were like agitators bawling a slogan, or massed troublemakers at a football match. But at the same time the noise was beginning to draw away. Gerald suspected that the entire population of the place was on the march.

Soon it was apparent that a processional route was being followed. The tumult could be heard winding about from quarter to quarter; sometimes drawing near, so that Gerald and Phrynne were once more seized by the first chill of panic, then again almost fading away. It was possibly this great variability in the volume of the sound which led Gerald to believe that there were distinct pauses in the massed shouting; periods when it was superseded by far, disorderly cheering. Certainly it began also to seem that the thing shouted had changed; but he could not make out the new cry, although unwillingly he strained to do so.

'It's extraordinary how frightened one can be,' said Phrynne, 'even when one is not directly menaced. It must prove that we all belong to one another, or whatever it is, after all.'

In many similar remarks they discussed the thing at one remove. Experience showed that this was better than not discussing it at all.

In the end there could be no doubt that the shouting had stopped, and that now the crowd was singing. It was no song that Gerald had ever heard, but something about the way it was sung convinced him that it was a hymn or psalm set to an out-of-date popular tune. Once more the crowd was approaching; this time steadily, but with strange, interminable slowness.

'What the hell are they doing now?' asked Gerald of the blackness, his nerves wound so tight that the foolish question was forced out of them.

Palpably the crowd had completed its peregrination, and was returning up the main street from the sea. The singers seemed to gasp and fluctuate, as if worn out with gay exercise, like children at a party. There was a steady undertow of scraping and scuffling. Time passed and more time.

Phrynne spoke. 'I believe they're *dancing*.'

She moved slightly, as if she thought of going to see.

'No, no,' said Gerald, and clutched her fiercely.

There was a tremendous concussion on the ground floor below them. The front door had been violently thrown back. They could hear the hotel filling with a stamping, singing mob.

Doors banged everywhere, and furniture was over-turned, as the beatic throng surged and stumbled through the involved darkness of the old building. Glasses went and china and Birmingham brass warming

75

pans. In a moment, Gerald heard the Japanese armour crash to the boards. Phrynne screamed. Then a mighty shoulder, made strong by the sea's assault, rammed at the panelling and their door was down.

'The living and the dead dance together.
Now's the time. Now's the place. Now's the weather.'

At last Gerald could make out the words.

The stresses in the song were heavily beaten down by much repetition.

Hand in hand, through the dim grey gap of the door-way, the dancers lumbered and shambled in, singing frenziedly and brokenly; ecstatic but exhausted. Through the stuffy blackness they swayed and shambled, more and more of them, until the room must have been packed tight with them.

Phrynne screamed again. 'The smell. Oh, God, the smell.'

It was the smell they had encountered on the beach; in the congested room, no longer merely offensive, but obscene, unspeakable.

Phrynne was hysterical. All self-control gone, she was scratching and tearing, and screaming again and again. Gerald tried to hold her, but one of the dancers struck him so hard in the darkness that she was jolted out of his arms. Instantly it seemed that she was no longer there at all.

The dancers were thronging everywhere, their limbs whirling, their lungs bursting with the rhythm of the song. It was difficult for Gerald even to call out. He tried to struggle after Phrynne, but immediately a blow from a massive elbow knocked him to the floor, an abyss of invisible trampling feet.

But soon the dancers were going again: not only from the room, but, it seemed, from the building also. Crushed and tormented though he was, Gerald could hear the song being resumed in the street, as the various frenzied groups debouched and reunited. Within, before long there was nothing but the chaos, the darkness, and the putrescent odour. Gerald felt so sick that he had to battle with unconsciousness. He could not think or move, despite the desperate need.

Then he struggled into a sitting position, and sank his head on the torn sheets of the bed. For an uncertain period he was insensible to everything: but in the end he heard steps approaching down the dark passage. His door was pushed back, and the Commandant entered gripping a lighted candle. He seemed to disregard the flow of hot wax which had already congealed on much of his knotted hand.

'She's safe. Small thanks to you.'

The Commandant stared icily at Gerald's undignified figure. Gerald tried to stand. He was terribly bruised, and so giddy that he wondered if this could be concussion. But relief rallied him.

'Is it thanks to *you*?'

'She was caught up in it. Dancing with the rest.' The Commandant's eyes glowed in the candlelight. The singing and the dancing had almost died away.

Still Gerald could do no more than sit upon the bed. His voice was low and indistinct, as if coming from outside his body. 'Were they . . . were some of them . . .'

The Commandant replied, more scornful than ever of his weakness. 'She was between two of them. Each had one of her hands.'

Gerald could not look at him. 'What did you do?' he asked in the same remote voice.

'I did what had to be done. I hope I was in time.' After the slightest possible pause he continued. 'You'll find her downstairs.'

'I'm grateful. Such a silly thing to say, but what else is there?'

'Can you walk?'

'I think so.'

'I'll light you down.' The Commandant's tone was as uncompromising as always.

There were two more candles in the lounge, and Phrynne, wearing a woman's belted overcoat which was not hers, sat between them, drinking. Mrs Pascoe, fully dressed but with eyes averted, pottered about the wreckage. It seemed hardly more than as if she were completing the task which earlier she had left unfinished.

'Darling, look at you!' Phrynne's words were still hysterical, but her voice was as gentle as it usually was.

Gerald, bruises and thoughts of concussion forgotten, dragged her into his arms. They embraced silently for a long time; then he looked into her eyes.

'Here I am,' she said, and looked away. 'Not to worry.'

78

Silently and unnoticed, the Commandant had already retreated.

Without returning his gaze, Phrynne finished her drink as she stood there. Gerald supposed that it was one of Mrs Pascoe's concoctions.

It was so dark where Mrs Pascoe was working that her labours could have been achieving little; but she said nothing to her visitors, nor they to her. At the door Phrynne unexpectedly stripped off the overcoat and threw it on a chair. Her nightdress was so torn that she stood almost naked. Dark though it was, Gerald saw Mrs Pascoe regarding Phrynne's pretty body with a stare of animosity.

'May we take one of the candles?' he said, normal standards reasserting themselves in him.

But Mrs Pascoe continued to stand silently staring; and they lighted themselves through the wilderness of broken furniture to the ruins of their bedroom. The Japanese figure was still prostrate, and the Commandant's door shut. And the smell had almost gone.

Even by seven o'clock the next morning surprisingly much had been done to restore order. But no one seemed to be about, and Gerald and Phrynne departed without a word.

In Wrack Street a milkman was delivering, but Gerald noticed that his cart bore the name of another town. A minute boy whom they encountered later on an obscure purposeful errand might, however, have been indigenous; and when they reached Station Road, they saw a small plot of land on which already men were silently at work with spades in their hands. They were as thick as flies on a wound, and as black. In the darkness of the previous evening, Gerald and Phrynne had missed the place. A board named it the New Municipal Cemetery.

In the mild light of an autumn morning the sight of the black and silent toilers was horrible; but Phrynne did not seem to find it so. On the contrary, her cheeks reddened and her soft mouth became fleetingly more voluptuous still.

She seemed to have forgotten Gerald, so that he was able to examine her closely for a moment. It was the first time he had done so since the night before. Then, once more, she became herself. In those previous seconds Gerald had become aware of something dividing them which neither of them would ever mention or ever forget.

Choice of Weapons

Fenville had never been to the Entresol before, but he took it to represent the kind of restaurant to which Ann was accustomed. Ann seemed pleased to go there: which was fortunate, because the excursion was a serious undertaking for Fenville, and only possible because more money than was customary had reached him from his mother that quarter. And then as soon as he had entered the place, certainly before they were seated at their table, he had fallen in love with someone else.

He first glimpsed this other person through a painted glass screen. The screen, glazed only in its upper part, separated the main area of the restaurant from an anteroom where drinks were brought to lacquered three-legged tables. While Ann was leaving her fur coat, Fenville sat at one of these tables warding off two solicitous youths in linen jackets. Right across the restaurant, which was not full, he saw this other woman seated alone at a table by the wall.

At present the distance, the shaded lights, and the fact that the glass in the screen was obscured by small bright flowers painted round its edges prevented Fenville from seeming to himself more than pleasantly disturbed; and when Ann returned he ordered drinks and consumed his own with what he took to be the aplomb their surroundings demanded.

Immediately he was beyond the screen, however, things were different, and he knew it. The bald head-waiter, pleased by Ann's softly luxurious appearance, led them the length of the room to a table against the far wall, and only three tables away from that occupied by the solitary woman. Even passing her table was for Fenville a strange ordeal.

Under-waiters began calling upon him to order, and such appetite as he might have had for the complex dishes listed had left him. Ann was talking to him more charmingly than ever before, but he was unable to respond to her skilful effort to lend him some of her own confidence. The wine itself, when it arrived, cased him in a shell of sobriety.

The woman at the other table he now saw was more truly to be described as a girl. She was younger even than Ann. She wore a topless black dress which made her shoulders and arms look more white and desirable than Fenville would have credited. She had a soft penumbra of hair tied with a black bow, and a small, sadly perfect face, with big, widely placed green eyes. Her hands fluttered about continuously, but she seemed to be eating as little as Fenville himself. Several courses arrived, lingered, and were removed, chilly, dispirited, intact. Fenville could hear her low musical voice as she addressed the waiters, but not her words. He was listening to her with pain in his heart as he tried to be attentive to Ann, under conditions to which in any case he was very unacclimatised. The other girl seemed quite assured, although the circumstances of her custom in the restaurant were surely unusual. Fenville noticed that she was not even drinking, which he had always understood to be a common complaint of waiters against women customers. On the other hand, she seemed unhappy; she was pale and unsmiling; and suddenly Fenville saw her produce a small gold bag and extract from it a minute wisp of handkerchief with which she touched one cheek, as if to blot out a tear.

Ann showed no sign of being aware how unused he was to fashionable restaurants, and continued to talk about what she was going to do when her studentship was successfully concluded. They were both studying architecture; and Fenville suspected that their professors considered Ann, favoured in so many ways, to be the more promising. He heard Ann saying that she would go into practice with a partner; that her father would give her all the capital she needed, and that it was simply a matter of finding the right person. He knew that Ann, whom a month ago he had hardly dared to speak to, and a week ago had thought he loved, was offering him a chance that was most unlikely ever to repeat itself: a whole life of common understanding and prosperity and security. But while she was gently amplifying the matter, the girl at the other table called for her bill.

Fenville sat staring at her. His hand shook so much that he could not hold the fork with which he had been trying to eat vol-au-vent. Ann stopped talking. Everybody else in the restaurant, which had begun to fill up, seemed to be shouting at the top of their voices. Ann touched his arm. It was the first time she had ever done so.

The other girl paid. The waiter bowed very low before her munificent tip, and pulled away the table. The girl drew a black silk scarf round her shoulders and rose. Mysteriously her scent reached Fenville for an instant.

'Mademoiselle has a coat?'

The girl shook her head, and began to walk away.

'I'll tell the porter to call mademoiselle a taxi.'

The girl shook her head more vigorously, and made a gesture as of pushing the waiter aside. She had reached the screen with the painted glass.

Fenville looked at Ann. His appearance made Ann not merely touch his arm but clutch at it. He drew himself away from her.

'Ann,' he said, 'forgive me. I'm so very sorry.' He could say no more, because by now the other girl would be out of the restaurant.

He fled from the table and pushed his way through a noisy business party which had just entered. There seemed to be at least a dozen of them, and Fenville trod upon their feet.

Outside, despite the waiter's solicitude, it did not seem cold. Fenville could see the girl walking along the street about a hundred yards away. Overwhelmed with relief at not having lost her, his mind became very clear. An immediate approach, he reflected would be disastrous. If, as was almost certain, he were rebuffed, she would walk out of his life. He resolved to follow her and discover where she lived.

At first the streets were crowded, and Fenville could see that people turned as she passed; but soon they reached a square which was almost empty, and Fenville could just hear her footsteps. She never looked back, but appeared to be using her hands to hold the big shawl in place over her head. The silhouette of her skirt projected on either side of her knees, and Fenville knew that were he closer he would hear it rustle.

She crossed Oxford Street, by which time Fenville was less than thirty yards behind her. On the north side she stopped and summoned a taxi. Fenville was little more used to taxis than to such restaurants as the Entresol, but he shouted for one which he saw in the distance, and told it to follow that which the girl had taken.

'What for?' asked the driver.

'For this,' replied Fenville, resourcefully pulling a pound note from the packet assigned to the entertainment of Ann.

The driver grabbed it.

'Get inside.'

Fenville was relieved by the alacrity of his acceptance. Preoccupied though he was, he began to realise that doors open to the rich.

Surprising also was the fact that the other taxi was still in sight. It had been mercifully delayed by the traffic lights.

'Hell of a street for this game,' remarked the taxi driver through his sliding window.

Fenville sat on the edge of the slippery seat, his gaze devouring the taxi ahead. If they were not to lose it, he too must keep his eyes on it.

Somewhere near the top of Bond Street, a boy fell off his bicycle. Fenville's taxi slowed.

'Go on,' shouted Fenville, his voice piping and strained.

The taxi failed to accelerate.

'Go on, you fool.'

The driver looked at Fenville, dissociating himself witheringly from what he plainly regarded as his lack of common decency, but said nothing, and went faster.

Fenville realised that the chase was made possible by the fact that the other taxi was not of the latest type. He came nearest to losing it when at the far end of Bays-water Road it turned into a Notting Hill side street.

But Fenville's driver found the right turn. Possibly he had more experience of the job in hand than Fenville had supposed. At the other end of the street, the girl was getting out.

'Stop,' cried Fenville.

The driver swore and stopped.

'I'm sorry,' said Fenville.

The driver said something unflattering. His mind was still upon the boy and the bicycle. He felt guilty because Fenville's money had made him overrule what he re-garded as his finer instincts.

Fenville alighted and waved the cab away. He was afraid it might not go. It was difficult for him to draw nearer, and the noise of his arrival might call the girl's attention to him. But the cabman clicked his flag, spat, and departed.

The difficulty now was to determine the exact house. The girl's taxi was also moving off, and she herself had vanished. They were shapeless, bulky houses, iced all over with elaborately decorated stucco. Every alternate mass was a single house, the others being pairs of houses gummed together. The night was overcast, the street slenderly lighted, and the windows muffled. Whereas, earlier, the girl's tapping heels had been hard to hear, now even the furtive footfalls of a darting cat stirred the patchy dimness. Fenville felt that he should tiptoe.

He walked slowly towards the region where the girl's taxi had come to rest. When he deemed that he was nearing the spot, he peered at each separate front door. The houses seemed identical: withdrawn, but only as if ashamed of their unfashionableness. Fenville began to panic and to walk faster. Better to complete the miserable business and not try to defer the admission of failure. Then he came to a house which was unlike the rest.

It was a single house, set further back than its neighbours, and even more substantial and elaborate. A shallow carriage-sweep led from each side to a columned porte-cochère, above which rose a line of decorative obelisks, miniatures of Cleopatra's Needle, and varying in size as if they were pieces in a game. On each side of this projecting porch were two smooth and polished sphinxes: half-tamed in order to guard the secrets within. Fenville saw that everywhere the stucco had been moulded into dusty images from Egypt and Assyria. The house might have been a provincial museum and art gallery; and it had a similar air of nocturnal inanimation.

Fenville moved on. The few houses beyond resembled those which had gone before. It was impossible to know which among eight or ten the girl had entered; and almost certainly impracticable to wait until she might again emerge. Fenville returned to the house with the porte-cochère, and seated himself on the rump of one of the domesticated sphinxes. He had nothing to lose by waiting at least until a policeman found him.

Within a few minutes he felt not only frustrated but frozen. He rose and began to pace up and down the pavement; but his quiescence had chilled him more than the exercise could warm him, especially in that he dared not extend his promenade beyond a short stretch of the street. Although doubtless the girl was now on her way to bed, she might, on the other hand, come out and turn in the opposite direction. Gradually, however, he began to enlarge his beat, until he was reversing at a spot fifty yards from the first house at which the girl's taxi could possibly have stopped.

He was nearing this point on one occasion when he heard a door bang. He swung round and saw that a man was coming towards him. Embarrassed, Fenville felt compelled to quicken his pace. The other man was also walking briskly, so that Fenville's observation of him was limited. When about twenty yards away, however, he passed beneath one of the dim street lights, and Fenville was startled. The man appeared to be in fancy dress. He wore a brown tailcoat, a frilled cravat, and narrow black trousers. He had dark, profusely curling hair falling on his neck, fine features, and a bearing which Fenville thought distinguished. As he passed he seemed for a second to glare at Fenville disdainfully. Beneath his arm was a stout cane with a long tassel.

Fenville could not but turn and look after him; but was mortified when in a second the man did the same thing. This time it was hard to doubt that the man was scowling at him. It was the man's appearance of hostility, in fact, which for a moment held Fenville's gaze, and presented him from instantly continuing on his way, as manners demanded. In the next moment, it became worse: the man seemed almost to snarl. Fenville turned, much shaken, walked rapidly past all the remaining houses, and out of the street. He caught a bus to his lodging, and wondered all night if he were going mad.

Earlier than usual the next morning, his landlady rapped at his door.

'Are you all right, Mr Fenville?'

Fenville had not slept, and now had heard her approaching slippers. He put on his dressing gown and opened the door. Most unexpectedly, Ann was standing in the passage behind her. She smiled at him.

'Miss Terrington's been telling me a long tale about you were taken ill last night,' said the landlady. 'You look all right to me.'

'Of course, I'm all right. Ann, come in. I must explain to you.'

'No visitors in bedrooms,' said the landlady. 'You know that as well as I do.'

'See you later?' asked Ann understandingly.

Fenville nodded.

But he had no idea what he could explain. He met the situation by absenting himself from the School of Architecture. He had no idea that he would ever see the other girl again, but he felt unable to face the kindness and imagination of Ann. The sensation of hopeless loss crunched through his nerves and froze his heart. Every simple movement required forethought and effort. Now and then, however, the image of the girl, the dire recollection of her voice and her scent and of the sound of her feet tapping across the square were replaced by the memory of the man who had passed him in the street, of his menacing expression, alert step, and strange costume.

The rules of the house would compel Fenville to leave it before ten o'clock, and he had nowhere to go. He told his landlady that after all he wasn't very well; and what he said gained credence from his manifest lack of appetite. An exemption was grudgingly made of him: he was permitted to remain in his room.

'But you must have a doctor.'

'I'm not as ill as all that.'

'Then you can't stay here.'

'All right. But I haven't got a doctor.'

'I'll send for Dr Bermuda. He's a specialist.'

'Truly, I don't need a doctor.'

But by the time Dr Bermuda appeared, Fenville was in such straits that he rose avidly to enquiries as to whether he was worried about anything. Dr Bermuda was an unkempt, sympathetic little man, made shapeless by stretching points in favour of his patients. Not only did Fenville tell the story of his love, but he also found a conscientious and expert listener. Once when the landlady rapped at the door, the Doctor cried out: 'Please, Mrs Stark. Apply yourself to your own duties, and leave me to mine.' Fenville realised that he had not heard her approaching, and deduced that she had been eavesdropping. He lowered his voice, even though he heard her shuffling away.

'I have no idea what to do next.'

'That's easy enough,' said Dr Bermuda. 'You go after her. The only way to get rid of a temptation is to yield to it.' He quoted gently, like an elderly country priest who sought no monsignorate but only to serve his tiny simple flock.

'But what can I do?'

The Doctor produced a large dingy wallet from the gaping inner pocket of his jacket, and from it extracted a card.

'The name of the street. Write it on the back.' He gave Fenville the card between his third and fourth fingers, tarry with nicotine; then laboriously stooped to gather up the cigarette papers he had let drift to the floor.

'I don't know the name of the street. I didn't notice.'

'Ah, you are still unaccustomed to romance. One soon learns.'

Fenville said nothing. He was too cast down even to resist this justified reflection upon his manhood.

Dr Bermuda rose fumblingly to his feet. 'Lie back,' he said.

'I don't want any further examination.'

'Back,' repeated the Doctor, with a short sharp flicker of his left hand. Fenville saw that he was wearing a big ring with a stone the colour of old-fashioned sugar candy. He lay back.

'Watch me,' said Dr Bermuda, waving his left hand, like a dwarfish policeman calling on traffic. 'Keep your eyes on mine.'

Fenville realised that he was being hypnotised; but it was too late to demur.

A moment later he was awake again, and the Doctor was writing on the card.

'Arcadia Gardens. Which end?'

'The far end,' said Fenville.

The Doctor looked at him.

'There's a house with sphinxes outside. *That* end.'

The Doctor stared into his eyes and wrote it down.

'How do you know I've got the right street?' asked Fenville.

'You noticed the name of it without being conscious of doing so. By modern science the suppressed memory has been recovered.'

'Suppressed? I didn't do that.'

The Doctor looked at him gravely. 'Didn't you?' he

said. 'A man in fancy dress? Who looked at you strangely? Whom you did not mention to me?' He raised his hand. Now it was as if he were stopping the traffic. 'I see you remember him.' Only the back of his ring was visible to Fenville. He became the physician giving orders. 'Do not leave the house until you hear from me again. I shall speak to Mrs Stark. I shall also speak to that other young woman; the one who so unluckily accompanied you to the restaurant. I must have her address too.' Fenville supplied it and the Doctor wrote it down. 'After that I shall institute some enquiries. We have resources nowadays for dealing with such matters. You may consider yourself to be dangerously ill; far more so than if you had a more conventional disease. Unless you meet this woman again and get to know her and masticate her and bite upon her and fully digest and eliminate her, you will be unlikely to recover. It is a rare disease you have; and fatal unless it is permitted to run its full course.' He smiled into his withered beard. 'Good-bye, my friend,' he said, drawing on his shabby brown leather gloves. 'Modern science will do its best to cure you.'

At half past twelve Mrs Stark brought luncheon: spaghetti au gratin, followed by ground rice and prunes, and a large white cup of piebald Camp coffee. At half past three, she reappeared with a letter. The writing was faint and shaky. The letter proved to be from the Doctor; written on his prescription paper.

'Her name is Dorabelle. Your magnetic undermind has already led you to her house. I have prescribed for

Miss Terrington. May eloquence attend you.' The Doctor enclosed his account for two and a half guineas.

By four o'clock Fenville could remain in bed no longer. Physical energy was wrestling with spiritual malaise. As the church clock struck, he rose and crept to the bathroom, there to shave in water which at that hour was scarcely tepid. He dressed and stole downstairs. In the hall he heard Mrs Stark snoring in her little back den. For many years the bottom of the front door had dragged on the lumpy linoleum, sometimes shaking the whole house; and now, as soon as Fenville had opened it, a gust of wind snatched it out of his hand and slammed it shut. He stood silent for a moment, but Mrs Stark's afternoon dreams were unbroken. At the second attempt, he was outside the house.

He walked through to Holborn and took a number 17 omnibus to Notting Hill. Then with some difficulty and several retracings of his path he made his way to the house with the sphinxes in Arcadia Gardens. As he walked between that noncommittal double file of portly residences, now, as he saw, divided and sub-divided within themselves, the wind lifted torn sheets of cheap newspaper, tossed in from other less desirable quarters, glanced at them, and blew them away. One of them tangled itself round Fenville's trousers. The street was empty and passé.

At the now-familiar front door, he rang the bell. More than once he lugged at the big iron knob without a sound reaching him. He began to shiver in the rising wind. But doubtless the bell had long since ceased to work. Then he heard slowly approaching steps. Their rhythm seemed to be erratic.

The door opened. A very tall, elderly man, with a pale, lined face, and dressed in black, spoke to Fenville.

'The tradesmen's entrance is round at the side.'

Fenville took a pull on himself. 'I want to see your mistress.'

The man looked at him. His aspect was so frail that he seemed in danger of blowing away.

Then he spoke in weary tones. 'There was another man last week.' He seemed resentful. Then he said, 'Wait a moment. I'll look in the almonry.'

He retreated into the gloom within. Fenville saw that he walked with difficulty. Soon he was back; and his long bony hand held a five-pound note.

'What's it for? Can't see what need there is for giving to charity nowadays.'

'I'm not collecting for charity,' said Fenville. 'I want to see your mistress. Is she in?'

'That's different,' replied the man sharply. 'You mean is she at home?'

Fenville realised that this was his first encounter with a butler.

'As you wish. Anyway I mean to see her.'

Again the man looked at him. 'Mean to see her, eh? What name?'

'Fenville.'

'Any business?'

Fenville hesitated.

But the man came to his rescue. 'Oh never mind,' he

said sulkily. 'I can't wait about all day in the cold.' And indeed he was beginning to cough. 'I'll have to shut the door.'

Fenville involuntarily withdrew half a step. Instantly the door was closed.

The man was gone for so long that Fenville was contemplating ringing again. His heart and pulses were all the time beating so fast that he felt he would be sick. He wondered whether he possessed the reserves for a second sortie. In the street beyond the encrusted porte-cochère, an old grey woman, stooped and shrouded and spent, was stumbling towards him against the wind. She seemed the female counterpart of the decrepit butler.

'Come in.' The door had re-opened a few inches, and its custodian spoke grudgingly through the crack. Fenville had to push it back. As soon as he was in, the door was shut again; and the butler moaning on about the cold.

Now that he was inside, Fenville was so completely unnerved that he was unable to speak. It was no moment for sympathetic small talk about the impact of the weather upon old blood.

'This way,' said the man, ungraciously as ever, and limped feebly forward.

The murky hall was in the same involved, derivative style as the exterior of the house, but here sustained in dark yellow stone. On the tiled floor was an immense rug, obviously once valuable, but now discoloured and torn. There was a large pyramidal fireplace, but no fire. Furniture was sparse, and what there was looked unused and dusty. A small chest stood open in a corner.

Behind the range of yellow columns to the left ascended a black wooden staircase. The butler slowly led the way, step by step drawing himself forward and upward by the immense moulded handrail. Fenville followed him. Two or three minutes seemed to pass before they reached the first landing. The stair carpet was as worn as the rug below, and there were no pictures on the walls. The house seemed extraordinarily draughty, until Fenville realised that several diamond panes were missing from the vast window which lighted the stairwell. The butler's cough became distressing. The stairs, it was clear, were not to be undertaken lightly. Fenville imagined that he should apologise for the trouble he was causing, but could find neither voice nor words.

At the top, where the stairs wound upwards to the second floor, a high cavernous passage, with the stairwell on one side, led past several panelled doors. At the end of the passage, the butler stopped, and feebly tapped at a door which was ajar.

Fenville heard no response, but response there must have been, for the butler pushed open the door with the length of his arm, and with his head motioned Fenville in.

'All right, Gunter,' said the voice which had been in Fenville's ears since the evening before. 'You can go.'

The door closed and Fenville was alone with the girl he was pursuing.

She sat in a corner of the high bay window behind an embroidery frame. The chair she occupied was so huge that it closely resembled an old-fashioned stage throne, and she a stripling queen. In this the chair was not alone: the room was big, and everything in it was big. The scale of even such small objects as the waste-basket and the coal scuttle made them very large objects. Unlike the hall and staircase, the room was ordered and warm.

'So you decided in favour of a formal call at the properly appointed hour.'

Fenville could only nod. She glanced at him and his eyes fell.

'Are you cold? Warm yourself before you try to talk.' Her hands were full of the accessories of her craft. She wore a brocaded dress which matched but bettered the room. Fenville drew near the roaring pyre on the palazzo-like hearth. For a minute there was no sound but that of the flames. Then the girl spoke again.

'What month is it?'

'October. But it seems colder than usual.'

Thus conventionally Fenville first addressed her.

'Sit down if you wish.'

'Thank you.' Fenville sat upon a stool with four carved and gilded legs and a patterned velvet seat. Half turning away from the girl, he cautiously extended his hands towards the flames.

'Don't you want to look at me?'

Fenville felt himself blushing all over his face and neck. The sensation was as painful as it was novel.

'It's no good coming to see me if you don't look at me.'

Fenville twisted round his legs to the other side of the

stool and regarded her. He now observed that the level of the floor in the bay window was considerably higher than in the rest of the room, so that he had to look up at her. She was working concentratedly.

'You can talk to me at the same time. But perhaps you're still warming yourself?' Her hands were fluttering about, as Fenville had seen them in the restaurant, but now with purpose.

'Thank you. I'm warm.'

'Would you like tea? You are paying me a formal call. I must respond. If you pull the bell, Gunter will appear – eventually.'

'I couldn't think of bringing him upstairs again.' Fenville was painfully aware that at Gunter's rate of progress, he could only just have reached the bottom of the flight.

She glanced at Fenville again and smiled. Instantly he felt that the two of them were alone together in the world. 'You're my guest,' she said. 'Look. The bell is behind you.'

There was no help for Gunter. Fenville turned and stared about.

'Look harder.'

Then Fenville realised. It was a bell of the earlier type with wires, and operated by a wide strip of thick yellow silk which hung from ceiling to floor in a corner of the projecting fireplace. He pulled it cautiously.

'Now you must *pull* harder.'

Fenville remembered the bell at the front door, and pulled very hard indeed.

'I can't hear anything.'

'Gunter can.'

'I hope I haven't damaged it.'

'You can't hurt bells like that. Only the modern electric ones. I'm sure you agree?'

'Yes. As a matter of fact I do.' Fenville had had many troubles with electric bells, partly because he did not understand electricity.

'That bell has never been repaired since the house was built.'

'How long ago was that?'

'Exactly a hundred years. I live in it because I can't afford to live anywhere else.'

'I see.' There was nothing else to say. Her eyes were fast on her work, and Fenville was staring at her.

'You know no one has any money any more?' The ungainly sentence was made music by her voice. Moreover she seemed to expect an answer.

'Neither I nor my family', said Fenville, gathering courage with the familiar reference, 'have ever had any money that I know of.'

'The other butlers in the Gardens have all become caretakers. At least I've saved Gunter from that.'

Fenville was wishing that Gunter would appear. Gunter's condition worried him. But conversation must be sustained.

'When I first arrived, Gunter thought I was collecting for charity and offered me five pounds.' He had meant to imply that this did not suggest penury in the house, but stopped short and again blushed.

'I keep up my father's almonry, naturally,' the girl said dispassionately; then raised her voice to bid Gunter come in. Fenville had been so occupied with her that he had after all missed Gunter's knock. 'Tea. At once, please.' Gunter mumbled something. 'At once, please.' Gunter withdrew. The girl had not looked up at him.

'Gunter seems a little under the weather. That cough . . .'

'I know he's slow. I'm sorry.'

It was not the aspect of Gunter's case which Fenville had in mind. But she spoke again.

'Do you often go to a restaurant with one woman and abandon her to chase another?'

'I could not help myself.'

'It was love at first sight?'

'I think it must have been.'

'If you are not certain, it wasn't. When it happened to me, I knew.'

Hardly believing his ears, Fenville softly said, 'I knew too.'

She put down her needle, and yawned slightly. 'Tell me,' she said, 'how do *you* pass the long hours of waiting?'

'I work. I'm an architectural student.'

'An architectural student dining at the Entresol?' She had risen and was coming towards him. Fenville caught his breath.

She did not seem particularly to expect a reply; but Fenville said peacefully, 'It was a special occasion.'

She sat down in one of the big armchairs and,

drawing up the wide sleeves of her dress, exposed her white forearms to the blaze. 'Was that your wife?'

'No,' said Fenville. 'Just a friend.'

'Ah, a rich girl, an heiress.' Fenville realised that this was not after all difficult to deduce. 'What a pity I'm not rich.'

Fenville gazed at her charming mouth, her young lashes, her soft skin, her perfect wrists, and miniature hands. 'You are beautiful.'

She made neither movement nor reply. She said, 'All the rooms in the house are different. Done by different designers: the best men of their day. This is the Quattrocento Room.'

'Yes,' said Fenville, glancing round. 'Will you show me the others?'

'The others are empty now. Locked up and shuttered. I've had to give up entertaining.'

'Did you entertain a lot?' She looked about nineteen or twenty.

'Every night. The house was never anything but full. That was when my father was alive, of course. I was hostess. Young though I was, he always preferred me to my mother. Then one night he shot himself, and I found we were ruined.'

'What a terrible thing! How long ago was this?'

'Oh I don't know. Years ago. My mother went mad. She was always unsophisticated, poor Mother. Father couldn't stand her in the room with him.'

'I see. I'm very sorry.' Fenville could think of nothing more to say.

'Yes,' the girl replied gravely. 'It's a tragedy to be poor.'

Fenville reflected. Again it was not the aspect of the matter which he had been thinking of. Staring at the huge lumps of blazing coal, he said, 'Have you ever considered coming out into the world?'

'I came out into the world only last night. I used to go to the Entresol with my father. I go there still whenever I want to think about him or ask his advice.'

'That was why you were sad?'

She gazed at him with her big brown eyes. 'I loved my father.' It seemed she might cry.

'Yes, of course. I'm being a fool.'

'And I needed him to tell me what to do.' She was still staring at Fenville, melting his heart and wits.

'But didn't you say he was dead?' The words were said before he had thought.

'He still tells me what to do when I'm in trouble. At least he usually does. Last night he didn't.' Her voice was full of bewilderment and regret. She slowly turned away her head.

She seemed to want, as one says, to 'talk about it', and the oddness of her remarks were for Fenville exceeded by their tenderness. 'I'm sorry you were disappointed,' he said.

But a new thought had struck her. 'Perhaps he sent *you* to advise me?' she cried. 'Instead of doing it himself. That would explain everything,'

'Perhaps it would,' replied Fenville, again rising to the obscure occasion.

'That was why you left your wife and followed me all the way home. I thought it was love, but it was something far more important. Dear Father!' She had clasped her hands together at her breast and her eyes were sparkling. There was a quality very juvenile also in her reference to something far more important than love.

'It *was* love,' cried Fenville, blushing again. 'And Ann is *not* my wife.'

'Ann?' She was looking at him almost with suspicion.

'Ann Terrington. My friend last night.'

'Oh yes, that country-looking girl.' She was so excited that she seemed to find difficulty in following her own train of thought. 'Do you think my father did send you here to be my friend?'

'I think he must have done.'

'I *need* a friend.'

Fenville smiled into her eyes. 'Here I am.'

'My friend! My friend!' She was clapping her hands and imitating a happy child. It was enchanting. Then her face changed and she said, 'Are you to be trusted?'

'Yes,' said Fenville steadily. 'I'm to be trusted.'

'With my heart?'

He stretched out his arm and touched her hand. She drew her hand away and said, 'But of course you know nothing about it.'

'You must tell me, Dorabelle.'

It had occurred to him that in support of the preposterous notion about her father was at least the curious intervention of Dr Bermuda.

'You know my name?' She looked genuinely startled. 'How do you know it?'

'As I love you, I made it my business to find out. And my name is Malcolm.'

She giggled. '"What's the boy Malcolm?"'

Although Fenville missed this reference, he liked her laughing at him. But she had a rather high laugh, which seemed unconnected with her normal voice, and which struck Fenville as much less beautiful.

'Where's tea? I'm going down to look.'

She flashed across the room like a kingfisher, and Fenville followed her along the cold passage and down the stairs.

'Really, Gunter doesn't deserve to work here another day. Look, he's left the almonry open.' She was pointing to the small chest in the hall.

'Shall I shut it?'

'And lock it. The key is never supposed to leave Gunter's chain.'

She was gone, presumably to the servants' quarters. Fenville walked across the torn and dingy hall carpet. Before locking the chest, he could not but look inside. It was packed tightly and systematically with wads of black-and-white Bank of England notes. Although it was not a large chest, there must have been many thousands of pounds in it. One wad, bound in red tape, lay loose on top of the rest. Fenville regarded the cache for a moment, thrust his hand and wrist deep into the packed, silky money, then, savouring the contact of the crisp paper, closed and locked the chest. He departed to look for Dorabelle.

There were many windy corridors, shut rooms, and alcoves walled up with cobwebs; but he could hear Dorabelle's voice in the distance, and found his way to it. The flagstones which floored the back premises were so uneven that Fenville thought it would be easy to trip and crack his skull.

When indeed he reached the vast square stony kitchen, he thought at first that something of the kind had happened to Gunter. The old man sat on a wooden chair with two spokes missing from its back, and leaned his head on a corner of the immense table. There was no sign of tea, and Dorabelle seemed to be railing at him.

'Here's the key,' said Fenville.

At the words Gunter raised his head, sat up, and feebly snatched the cold object. He drew a key ring on the end of a chain from his trousers pocket and began to pick at it with his clumsy, bony fingers.

'We shall have to get tea ourselves,' said Dorabelle. 'Gunter is fit for nothing this afternoon. It is a disgrace when a visitor pays me a formal call.'

Gunter continued weakly to fiddle with the ring.

'Better let me do it,' said Fenville, depressed and rattled by the sight.

Dorabelle stood silently watching him as, none too adroit with key rings himself, he slowly went through the necessary motions, splitting a fingernail in the process.

'Will you kindly help with tea also?'

'Yes, of course,' said Fenville hastily, turning his back

upon the supine Gunter. 'What shall I do?'

'Everything, I'm afraid,' said Dorabelle. 'I'm not accustomed to doing housework.' Then she added, 'Isn't the kettle boiling?'

It was an enormously heavy and capacious iron object, mounted on an antique coal 'range'. The fire in the range was so low that Fenville could only suppose that the kettle had been on all the afternoon. Fenville made the tea in a mighty silver pot which stood surrounded by boat-like cups on the monumental dresser.

He looked round for food. There was a number of cupboards, with wooden doors painted in yellowing white. He opened one: and immediately shut it. All the shelves were piled not with grocery and provisions but with wads of bank notes, like those in the hall chest.

It was by no means the largest of the cupboards, but Fenville did not venture upon another. He said. 'I've made the tea. What happens next?'

Dorabelle was standing at the other end of the big, bare kitchen table. She was looking at Gunter with an expression of hostile curiosity.

'We'd better go back. There are some sweet biscuits upstairs.'

Fenville placed the silver teapot, the silver milk jug, the silver sugar basin, and two cups on an ornate and weighty silver tray, and followed her to the Quattrocento Room. Here she produced a robust silver biscuit barrel and offered it to Fenville. It contained biscuits about five inches in diameter and at least half an inch in thickness. They bore no maker's name, and proved to taste of aniseed.

'I am going to tell you everything,' said Dorabelle, sipping tea from her large flat cup. 'It is my father's wish.'

'Yes,' said Fenville. 'I think you'd better.' After all, she had as good as said that she loved him.

'I'm in love. Terribly in love.'

Fenville smiled fondly at her.

'Much more than you.'

Fenville shook his head.

'It began just after my father died.'

Fenville put down his cup, spilling the tea.

'I don't know his name.'

Fenville looked at the floor, his heart like a stone round his neck. 'I misunderstood you,' he said. 'It was my fault. I don't think you'd better go on.'

'Oh, but I must go on. No one else knows. You will tell me what to do.' Again her eyes were full of lights. Her hands fluttered in her lap, like newly born doves.

Fenville made a despairing gesture of acquiescence. Seated intimately behind the tea tray, she looked more charming and attractive than ever.

'There's a big looking glass. It used to be in the Versailles Room. I hid it when the other things went. In the end I put it in my bedroom.'

Curiously enough Fenville had not considered the question of where she slept.

'I used to look at myself in it for hours on end. And then one night I wasn't there.'

'You mean you were away?' It would probably be as

well to listen sympathetically. There might be pickings of comfort and stealings of hope.

'No, no, of course not. I never go away. I was going to bed one night – ' her eyes were cast inward upon the memory – 'and I looked in the glass and there was no one there.'

For the first time it occurred clearly to Fenville that she might be a little deranged.

'That was all. I thought I was going mad. I shut my eyes. Oh, for a long time. When I dared to open them again, I was back in the glass.'

'I expect you were overtired.'

She smiled: an exquisite smile of climax and revelation. 'When I looked the next night, *he* was there.'

It dawned on Fenville that this was no true rival at all. The relief of it. 'Tell me,' he said encouragingly.

'I had only just entered the room. In fact the first I saw of him was merely a glance over my shoulder. Then I looked full in the glass. I wasn't there: and he *was*. I loved him at first sight, just as you did me. I don't suppose you'd be here now, if he hadn't taught me how to love at first sight.'

'What did he look like?'

'He's about the same age as me and terribly handsome of course, especially when he wears fancy dress. He does sometimes. He's dreadfully vain.' She smiled contentedly.

For Fenville's latest hopes a bell began to toll. 'What sort of fancy dress?' he asked.

'The sort that makes men look good. Eighteenth

century, with a powdered wig. Or Regency buck. Oh, he knows how to make the most of himself.'

Fenville's cup was empty, but she did not offer to refill it.

'Do you talk to him?'

'Yes, of course. He talks wonderfully.'

'But you said you didn't know his name?'

'He'll only tell me if I agree to marry him.'

'You can hardly marry a man who lives in a mirror and whose name you don't know,' said Fenville primly.

'Of course I could. It would be the only kind of man I ever *could* marry. My father would have known that.' She glared at him in proud disappointment. For a moment it struck Fenville that she had picked up that hard look from the baleful lover. Then her face softened. 'But there *is* a difficulty. That's what I want advice about. *Please* advise me.'

'All right.' She seemed quite to forget that he, Fenville, might have some rights of his own in the matter. Then he recollected that indeed presumably he had none.

She went on raptly. 'He will insist that I'm an heiress. He's too silly about it. He keeps on saying the house is lined with money. As if I didn't know what was in my own house. That,' she said, entering a side issue, 'was why I was so careful to make things clear to *you* from the first.'

'Yes,' said Fenville. 'Thank you. And the point is that you don't want to marry a fortune-hunter?'

'Not at all. If I married him, I should naturally give him everything. But I don't want him to marry me thinking I've a lot of money when really I've nothing.'

'But if you keep telling him—'

'He won't listen.' Her small hands were clenched.

Fenville was about to say 'Then he'd better take his chance,' but managed to stop himself. There was no point in handing his rival victory on a plate. He said, 'I don't think his obstinacy promises well for matrimony.'

She looked at him sharply. Apparently she was impressed.

'There's the thing about his name as well,' said Fenville, pressing on.

'I don't *want* to know his name.'

Suddenly Fenville's eye lighted upon something. Behind Dorabelle, in a corner of the platform upon which the embroidery frame stood, rested a stout cane with a long tassel. It fixed his attention. He became very frightened. About the tasselled cane there seemed to be a distinctive evil of a nightmare, hopeless to resist. He could not drag his eyes from it.

'I love him so much,' said Dorabelle dreamily. 'But I don't think I should marry him on false pretences.'

'No,' said Fenville in a different tone, and trying to gather himself together. 'I don't think you should. In fact I'm quite sure you shouldn't.'

'He's the only one who will ever make me entirely happy,' she said.

'You can't know that.'

'You know very well you can know.'

There was a pause. 'Is there anything else you want advice about?' asked Fenville, striving for normality.

'What are you looking at?' She glanced over her shoulder, following the direction of his eyes. 'Oh, my embroidery. It gives me something to do while waiting for *him*.'

Fenville spoke very quietly. 'Does he come in here?'

'No. The glass is always between us, although often it is very thin. Like a film before the eyes. Sometimes it seems to vanish altogether, but then I know that I am dreaming, and sure enough in the end I wake up . . . No,' she said more steadily, 'I don't want any more advice. I feel it is not disinterested.'

'I think it is.'

'I don't believe it was my father who sent you at all.'

'I never said it was.' Fenville immediately regretted the cheap retort.

'It is getting late. You must go.' She was looking about her.

'May I come and see you again?'

'If you wish.'

'Can I come tomorrow?'

'Would that please you?'

'Of course.'

'Well then come tomorrow. Now look at my embroidery. I have worked at it for so long.'

Repugnance for that part of the room was very strong in Fenville, but he had to follow her. He stepped on to the platform, keeping the tasselled cane in view all the time.

'At least I've made a lovely pattern.'

With much of his attention elsewhere, Fenville

looked at the frame. Immediately he was even more frightened than before. There was no pattern at all but only a tangle of loose ends, a melee of different coloured silks.

'Don't you think it's pretty?' Dorabelle's tone was that of a schoolgirl coquettishly soliciting attention.

He was taller than she, and she gazed up at him. 'I don't think you do,' she said; and said no more about it. Fenville could say nothing.

She politely saw him out. There was no further sign of Gunter. Dusk was falling.

She was about to open the front door. Then she changed her mind and stood with her back to it. 'Come again,' she said. 'I like being loved at first sight.' Swiftly she kissed Fenville on the mouth. It was perhaps the most unexpected thing of all, and certainly the most disastrous. Then he was outside.

He could not sleep. He could not eat. He could in no way systematise what he had seen and heard.

'Good afternoon, Gunter,' he said the next day. It was half an hour earlier than his previous visit.

Gunter made no response.

'You look better.' The strange thing was that Gunter really did. He moved with more alacrity, and breathed without wheezing. Moreover his hands no longer shook. Only his attitude seemed unchanged.

'You know the way up,' he said, cast an odd sidelong look at Fenville, and positively hopped off to his solitary kitchen.

Fenville noticed that the 'almonry' had disappeared.

He ascended the dismal stairs and knocked at the door of the Quattrocento Room.

Dorabelle was sitting in the big armchair by the fire. There was no sign of the tasselled cane.

'Enter Malcolm with Drum and Colours.'

She was wearing the same dress; but she was surrounded by a cocoon of soft, black, gauzy material, upon which she was plying her needle.

Yesterday Fenville had been filled with insane courage. Today he felt exhausted and abashed.

'So Gunter wouldn't show you up?'

'He said I knew the way. I do, of course.'

'The reason servants open doors is not because their masters can't open them themselves. No, no, Gunter has been discharged.'

Fenville was sitting opposite her. Even in less than twenty-four sleepless hours he had forgotten the splendid details of her beauty. The rediscovery of them temporarily appeased the raw hunger of his nerves.

'Surely Gunter didn't behave as badly as all that?'

'It wasn't anything he did.' She laughed her slightly discordant laugh; the one blemish in her exquisiteness. 'I've become engaged to be married, and my future husband has servants of his own.'

Fenville wanted very much to cry. The struggle not to do so paralysed his tongue and throat muscles.

'I decided, you see, to disregard your advice.'

She continued sewing for a moment in silence. The black gauze reached up from her lap, beyond her left shoulder, and over the back of the high chair, like a spectre.

'I can't expect you to congratulate me.'

'I don't think I know you well enough,' said Fenville bitterly.

'Surely we are old friends?'

Fenville said nothing.

'Only an old friend could advise so badly.' She spoke flippantly, and as if Fenville really were an old friend.

'I saw him once,' said Fenville harshly. 'This man of yours. I hope that surprises you. I didn't like the look of him.'

Of course he was behaving like a fool. Certainly she did not seem at all surprised or even offended.

'I like the look of him more than anything in the world.'

'He's bad,' said Fenville, amazed by his pointless uncouthness.

'And you're good?' She stared at him questioningly, as if the idea had struck her for the first time.

'Better than he is.'

She looked away and laughed her alien laugh. 'You must have heard that love doesn't go by deserts.'

Fenville had heard it but until now had never believed it.

'That's only friendship,' she said. 'Quite different.'

'Friendship between us is out of the question.' Having fired the first of his boats, Fenville was not watching the whole fleet burn.

'How young you are!'

Of course she was substantially the younger of the two. As usual when he was with her, Fenville knew that he was blushing.

She disentangled hersef from her work and came and sat at his feet.

She took his hands. 'You must come and see me whenever you wish.'

'Why should I come and see you after you're married to someone else?'

'If you really love me, as I know you do, you won't want to stop seeing me because of that. You would only do that if it was yourself you loved and not me.'

This unexpectedly shrewd remark disconcerted Fenville and, unused as he was to serious affairs of the heart, might have planted a real doubt.

'I do love you.' He was choked and bemused by it, as by poison gas.

'If you don't come, I shall hate you.'

Still holding his hands, she gazed at him, unsmiling and mysterious. Looking down at her he could see her white breasts inside her loose brocaded dress. Nothing he could do could prevent him lifting her up and covering her face and neck with kisses.

She neither responded nor resisted. Fenville's soaring of passion began at length to dip earthwards. But he clasped her in his arms, and at once she began violently to tremble. To Fenville it was as if the life force itself were shaking her: the contrast with her previous passivity was more than he could bear. He sank his lips in her hair and muttered incoherent endearments. He was lost alike to the world and to all cognisance of what she thought or felt.

Then, as by a lightning-stroke, she was severed from him. He saw her standing with her hands behind her clutching the high column of the fireplace, her hair wild, her lips parted, her eyes like green fire.

He realised that the door was opening.

He was at first too abashed to turn and look behind him. But in an instant Dorabelle had relaxed into her customary stature of authority. It was only Gunter, and what he said constituted the vilest anticlimax.

'I want a hand with my things.' He sounded as sulky as ever.

Dorabelle's rejoinder was alarming. She stretched to the wide overmantel and grasped the familiar tasselled cane. It had been lying there out of sight. There was an expression of rage on her face which Fenville had never seen on any face before. It terrified him and also rallied him.

He put a hand on Dorabelle's arm which held the cane. 'I'll come down,' he said over his shoulder to Gunter.

At once he got the impression that Dorabelle's rage was transferred to him. It was as if she were silently but effectively destroying him as he stood.

He dropped his hand and took a step back. Then he turned and confronted Gunter. Here too in its way was a surprise. Gunter was dressed almost smartly, and looked a new man. There was something unreasonable about the change in him.

Without looking back Fenville followed Gunter down to the hall. Gunter's luggage consisted in a battered cabin trunk and three large boxes made of shiny black metal. A taxi driver was regarding the heap disconsolately. Fenville had not altogether expected Gunter to be departing by taxi.

He lifted an end of one of the tin boxes.

"Opeless,' said the taxi driver, his cloth cap on the back of his head.

'What's in it?' said Fenville involuntarily.

'Papers,' replied Gunter with some rancour.

'Come on,' said Fenville to the taxi driver. 'We'll do it between us.'

And they did. Although Fenville did not care for the job at all, he and the taxi driver stowed the three boxes, while Gunter stood by. The cabin trunk was lighter, and the taxi driver was able to manage it on his own. Then Gunter, without a word of thanks, but, to Fenville's mind, almost horribly spry, hardly limping at all, stepped in, and the taxi drove slowly off. The driver had seemed almost to be looking to Fenville for a gratuity in advance.

Filled with distracting hopes and fears, Fenville returned upstairs. Nothing would have much surprised him, except what he found. The room was empty. That he had not thought of.

He took a few steps inside, then stopped. All around Dorabelle's empty chair was the black fluffy gauze. Now Fenville perceived its purport. Dorabelle was making of it her wedding veil. He saw a little black wreath, the size of her head.

For a moment he was unable to move, but stood staring at the stuff, bewildered and horrified. Then he walked backwards to the door. He glanced about him.

'Dorabelle!'

But his voice had left him. He was croaking ridiculously.

The light from the room fell wanly autumnal on the passage where he stood. Out there he had never before really looked about him. Now he saw that the house was even worse kept than he had thought: a horrid orange-coloured fungus had sprouted on one of the carved wooden uprights which supported the landing rail, and the floor, uncarpeted beyond the staircase, was submerged by a stagnant tide of dust. Inside the room the huge fire noisily exalted and devoured; but here in the cold, Fenville could see his footprints, and what he took to be the larger ones of Gunter.

He stole along the landing to the stair, where again he stood and listened. He thought he heard someone moving quietly about on the floor above him. Swiftly and silently he descended. When he opened the front door, he received another surprise. Again there was a vehicle outside. He certainly had not heard it draw up.

'Good evening, young shepherd.'

It was a large, ancient Daimler, and the time-worn head of Dr Bermuda addressed him facetiously from the back window.

'How did you know?' asked Fenville.

A stunted youth, dressed in black, had come down from the driver's seat and was opening the rear door. Fenville was so eager to get away from the house that immediately he stepped inside. The youth returned to his place, and they slipped silently into Arcadia Gardens.

'My son,' said Dr Bermuda, indicating the driver. 'And my assistant. In my specialist work only, of course.'

'How did you know I was here?' repeated Fenville.

'Even though professionally you are concerned with the arts and not the sciences,' replied Dr Bermuda, 'you must have heard that free will has at last been proved an illusion.'

'I wasn't thinking in terms of philosophy.'

'Why should you?' enquired the Doctor, in his soft voice, weary with well doing. 'It is not a matter for philosophy, but for a more exact science. I specialise – what time I have to specialise at all – in the science of the mind. The *science* of the mind, I point out.'

'Nor,' said Fenville, 'do I want the attentions of a psychologist. If you don't mind.'

'Naturally not,' replied Dr Bermuda, all understanding. 'Patients who need us seldom want us.'

The lights were coming on in the Bayswater Road.

After a pause, Fenville said, 'I don't need you either. I'm cured.'

'What could be more satisfactory?' asked Dr Bermuda mildly.

'The whole thing was nothing but imagination.'

'Even as a layman you can hardly expect there are

exceptions to *that* rule.'

'I'll send you my cheque.'

In the dusky corner of the car the Doctor made a gesture which implied that he had at one time been educated out of England.

Conversation lapsed. Refusing to cast even a glance inside himself, Fenville sat obliquely regarding the weedy back of the Doctor's son. The boy's ears were unequal in size, and his hair was tufty and unprofuse.

'He is the apple of my eye,' remarked the Doctor, who did indeed seem to have the power of following his patient's thoughts. 'He will be a far greater scientist than I am.'

Fenville felt that this called for an indication of scepticism, but he said nothing.

'I have had to waste too much time in more general practice. Scientific harlotry.'

They had reached Marble Arch. The cinema queues were beginning to flinch and stamp. Unexpectedly the car turned up a side street to the left. It was quite enough to disarrange Fenville's unreal calm.

'Where are we going?' His voice evinced panic and dread.

The Doctor looked at him for a moment. A street light showed his wise, tired eyes.

'Home,' said the Doctor. 'Where else?'

'This isn't the usual way.'

'My son,' said the Doctor proudly, 'knows all the short cuts.'

*

Immediately he entered his unlovely room Fenville knew that his brief anaesthesia was ended. He had known that of course it must end before long; but had expected it to last longer than it had, if only in proportion to the shocks which had caused it. Within a minute of the door being shut, frustrated passion and confused terror were once more upon him, mangling his brain. It was almost as if Dr Bermuda had indeed been a steadying influence.

He sat upon his high stool and sank his head upon his small, second-hand drawing desk. The gas fire was un-lighted, and he had hardly eaten for three days.

After an uncertain interval there was a knock at his door. Fenville made no response.

The door was gingerly opened.

'Why ever don't you put the light on, Mr Fenville?'

Mrs Stark repaired the omission. Fenville found that his very muscles were congealed into despair.

'Don't you want any supper?' Supper was an extra.

'No thank you, Mrs Stark.'

'You can't expect to get better if you don't do what the Doctor says.'

'I don't expect to get better.' As so often, he spoke his thought without discretion.

Mrs Stark looked at him balefully. 'Then you'll have to live somewhere else. I'm not matron of a hospital.' This put her in mind of her real business. 'Don't suppose you even knew about Miss Terrington?'

'What about her?' Fenville had hardly given a thought to Ann since the Doctor's reference to her in his note.

'Made away with herself. Overdose of stuff to make her sleep. You've got a lot to do with it if you ask me.' Mrs Stark crossed her arms in order to pass judgment.

Fenville sank upon his bed.

'You've every right to look upset. Weren't you engaged to her? By what I've seen I'm sure I hope you were.'

Fenville's mind was upon Ann's love of life and upon the Doctor's routine words: 'I have prescribed for Miss Terrington.'

'When did it happen?' he said in a low voice. 'How do you know about it?'

'It happened yesterday. It's in all the papers.' She looked at him more malevolently than ever. 'What have you been doing with yourself, Mr Fenville, that you haven't even seen a paper?'

'I often don't see a paper.' But plainly for Mrs Stark such a statement was hard to believe. 'Is there going to be an inquest?'

'Of course there's going to be an inquest.' The whole framework of society found in her an oracle.

'I don't believe she killed herself for a moment.'

'Miss Terrington didn't strike me as the kind to have an accident.'

'Accidents can happen to anyone,' replied Fenville, forlornly. He was thinking of his visit to the Entresol.

That night he fell into a heavy sleep as soon as he got into bed. He dreamed that he was being married to Dorabelle in a vast sooty building lighted by numberless glowworms embedded in the soot. At the climax of the service a hand fell from behind on his shoulder and Fenville awoke. He could still feel the hand, and saw that a nightlight was burning by his bedside. He was unable to account for this attention: it was exceedingly unlike Mrs Stark. Possibly, he reflected, the Doctor had given orders.

The grip of the dream hand was weakening, as if a real hand were in dissolution. Fenville sat up, his thoughts tearing at his throat. Under the nightlight was a piece of paper. He pulled it out, and just managed to read it. It simply read, 'I want you.'

Fenville got out of bed and turned on the electric light. The paper was pale blue, and embossed at the top was a pale blue sphinx. There was no signature.

He dragged on his clothes like a criminal, and faltered out of the house. He was a little surprised to see that a light still burned in Mrs Stark's cubby-hole; which also exuded a smell of charred bloaters. Outside he looked at his watch. It was twenty minutes to two.

It was drizzling slightly, so that Fenville half ran through the back streets to Holborn. There he saw an all-night bus going in his direction, which, by a lung-bursting sprint, he managed to catch. He heard the conductress passing an unfavourable comment on his appearance to the man seated confidentially by the door.

At Notting Hill the rain stopped, but at the top of Arcadia Gardens Fenville was addressed by a policeman on his beat.

'Everything all right?'

'Of course.'

'Live round here?'

'Yes,' said Fenville; then foreseeing the next question, changed his mind. 'No. I live off Holborn.'

'You're going the wrong way.'

'Can't I go which way I like?'

Perhaps this made the policeman decide that Fenville was harmless. 'I only said you're going the *wrong* way,' he said and resumed his patrol.

Fenville had been wondering if Dorabelle herself would open the door. This did not happen: the very instant he had pulled the big iron bell-handle, the door swung wide and Fenville saw the man in fancy dress. His handsome shape stood out against a background of lighted candles in massive silver candlesticks.

Instantly Fenville drew back, but it was useless. The man's arm shot out, and dragged him in. It was elegantly done, like a move in ju-jitsu. Then the man had shut the door and was standing with his back to it.

'Thief!' The man's voice was deep and musical.

Fenville could think of nothing to say.

'Thief!' said the man again.

'What have I stolen?' But Fenville knew the question was useless; because he already knew the answer. His wits made incandescent by danger, he saw the significance of the missing 'almonry', realised that much else was doubtless missing.

'It was Gunter,' he cried. 'I am sure it was Gunter.'

'Coward also,' said the man. It was a simple statement of fact.

Fenville tried to pull himself together. 'I had nothing whatever to do with it,' he said. An endless line of indicted men stretched before his mind, all making the same assertion.

'Then,' said the man, 'you will fight.' Again it was a statement of fact. 'You may have the choice of weapons,' he added sneeringly, and lifted the tasselled cane from a broken chair.

Now it so happened that Fenville's father had been an amateur fencer in his youth, and had given his son a few lessons.

'Don't be absurd,' said Fenville. 'Don't take fancy dress too far.'

The man's face did not change. 'There are rapiers,' he said, 'behind the clock. Or pistols in my bedroom.'

'Rapiers,' said Fenville. His idea was to corner his antagonist, and contrive his own escape. Strangely, his heart was rising.

The man locked the front door and threw the key on the high mantelpiece above Fenville's head. Fenville heard it strike one of the heavy candlesticks. Then the man strode lightly over to a tall clock, the size of a sentry box and long silent. In an instant he had thrown it to the floor, where it fell with a terrifying, echoing crash, scattering glass and rusted spidery springs. Then he stood with a discoloured rapier in his hand.

'Can you catch?' he enquired brutally, and cast the rapier at Fenville's head. Oddly enough, Fenville could catch, although he injured one of his fingers on the metal hilt.

The ruined clock lay between them. The man appeared to have no weapon but his thick cane; then he made a movement, and Fenville realised that the cane was a swordstick. The next second the man had crossed the clock and was attacking. Fenville could see the tasselled sheath lying on the torn carpet behind him.

The man was fighting with wild ferocity, light on his feet and diabolically quick of eye. Fenville found time to be astonished by the viability of his own defence; but he was rapidly forced to the staircase end of the hall, and then, in order to gain ground, up the stairs themselves.

Not only the hall but the staircase, and indeed, as it seemed, the whole house, were illuminated by the candles in silver candlesticks: Fenville, amateurishly defending himself, retreated upwards step by step between two tiers of them. The other man fought silently and methodically, his firm lips just parted before his sharp teeth.

Their weapons tapped like the castanets of death. The momentary elation was over: this was the reckoning.

Fenville knew that he could not last much longer. In another minute, or perhaps two, the strange, impossible fight would be ended, and with it his life. Then an idea came to him. He leaped backwards up the two remaining steps to the almost familiar landing; hurled one of the candlesticks with his left hand into the other man's face; and in the instant passed his rapier right through his body. The other man dropped backwards without a word and with a momentous thud: and Fenville himself sagged unconscious to the floor.

When he came round, the misty eyes of Dr Bermuda looked into his.

'Try to stand,' said the Doctor. 'There's very little time.' His face was fraught with grave tidings.

Fenville found that one of the big chairs had been drawn from Dorabelle's room, and he seated on it. This time he did not trouble to ask the Doctor how he came to be there. The Doctor's undersized son was shambling about in the background.

'Try to walk,' said the Doctor to Fenville. 'You are in no way injured.'

Fenville crossed to the landing rail and looked downwards. There was no sign of the body. For the first time he noticed that the floor was littered with stale confetti.

'This way,' said the Doctor. 'Come with me.'

Fenville followed the trail of confetti.

On the long gilt sofa before her fire, lay Dorabelle. The light of many candles shone on her white face and wild hair. She had been wrapped in a blanket, but already the blanket was stained with blood from her breast . . . Singularly, Fenville was not surprised: Dorabelle had herself told him; and part of his brain, what the Doctor might have called his magnetic undermind, had known all along.

'You must be quick,' whispered the Doctor in his ear. Then, beckoning away his attendant son, he left them together.

Fenville sank upon his knees and lightly touched Dorabelle's lips. Her lovely arms lay outside the blanket, and she was able to wind them about his neck.

'Darling,' she said. 'My only love.'

As once before, he kissed her frenziedly. This time she seemed to respond; and Fenville was swept by a hysterical surge of joy. He kissed her again and again; until he realised that her lips and throat were cold, and that she was dead beneath his kisses.

Tired beyond tears, he sank his cheeks on her spoilt body. He heard a thumping at the front door below; and presently a voice spoke beside him.

'Dad says its the police.'

Fenville looked up, his face blotched with Dorabelle's blood.

But Dr Bermuda stood in the doorway.

'Modern science', he said, 'has failed to cure you; but she will not leave you to the outmoded harlequinade of the law.' He smiled tenderly and again beckoned his son. 'Go to the bedroom,' he said. 'Look behind the mirror. Bring what you find. And hurry.'

The Waiting Room

Against such interventions of fate as this, reflected Edward Pendlebury, there was truly nothing that the wisest and most farsighted could do; and the small derangement of his plans epitomised the larger derangement which was life. All the way from Grantham it had been uncertain whether the lateness of the train from King's Cross would not result in Pendlebury missing the connection at York. The ticket inspector thought that 'they might hold it'; but Pendlebury's fellow passengers, all of them businessmen who knew the line well, were sceptical, and seemed to imply that it was among the inspector's duties to soothe highly strung passengers. 'This is a Scarborough train,' said one of the businessmen several times. 'It's not meant for those who want to go further north.' Pendlebury knew perfectly well that it was a Scarborough train: it was the only departure he could possibly catch, and no one denied that the timetable showed a perfectly good, though slow, connection. Nor could anyone say why the express was late.

It transpired that the connection had not been held.

'Other people want to get home besides you,' said the man at the barrier, when Pendlebury complained rather sharply.

There were two hours to wait; and Pendlebury was

warned that the train would be very slow indeed. 'The milk-and-mail we call it,' said his informant.

'But it does go there?'

'In the end.'

Already it was late at night; and the refreshment room was about to close. The uncertainty regarding the connection had made Pendlebury feel a little sick; and now he found it difficult to resume reading the Government publication the contents of which it was necessary for him to master before the next day's work began. He moved from place to place, reading and rereading the same page of technicalities: from a draughty seat under a light to a waiting room, and, when the waiting room was invaded by some over-jolly sailors, to the adjoining hotel, where his request for coffee seemed to be regarded as insufficient.

In the end it was long before the train was due when he found his way to the platform from which his journey was to be resumed. A small but bitterly cold wind was now blowing through the dark station from the north; it hardly sufficed to disturb the day's accumulation of litter, but none the less froze the fingers at a touch. The appearance of the train, therefore, effected a disproportionate revival in Pendlebury's spirits. It was composed of old stock, but none the less comfortable for that; the compartment was snugly heated, and Pendlebury sat in it alone.

The long journey began just in time for Pendlebury to hear the Minster clock clanging midnight as the train slowly steamed out. Before long it had come to rest again, and the bumping of milk churns began, shaking the train as they were moved, and ultimately crashing, at stately intervals, to the remote wayside platforms. Observing, as so many late travellers before him, that milk seems to travel from the town to the country, Pendlebury, despite the thuds, fell asleep, and took up the thread of anxiety which he so regularly followed through the caves of the night. He dreamed of the world's unsympathy, of projects hopefully begun but soon unreasonably overturned, of happiness filched away. Finally he dreamed that he was in the South of France. Although he was alone, it was beautiful and springtime; until suddenly a bitter wind descended upon him from nowhere, and he awoke, hot and cold simultaneously.

'All change.'

The door of the compartment was open, and a porter was addressing him.

'Where are we?'

'Casterton. Train stops here.'

'I want Wykeby.'

'Wykeby's on the main line. Six stations past.'

'When's the next train back?'

'Not till six-thirty.'

The guard had appeared, stamping his feet.

'All out please. We want to go to bed.'

Pendlebury rose to his feet. He had cramp in his left arm, and could not hold his suitcase. The guard pulled it out and set it on the platform. Pendlebury alighted and the porter shut the door. He jerked his head to the guard, who clicked the green slide of his lantern. The train slowly steamed away.

'What happens to passengers who arrive here fast asleep?' asked Pendlebury. 'I can't be the first on this train.'

'This train's not rightly meant for passengers,' replied the porter. 'Not beyond the main line, that is.'

'I missed the connection. The London train was late.'

'Maybe,' said the porter. The northerner's view of the south was implicit in his tone.

The train could be seen coming to rest in a siding. Suddenly all its lights went out.

'Casterton is quite a big place, I believe?'

'Middling,' said the porter. He was a dark-featured man, with a saturnine expression.

'What about a hotel?'

'Not since the Arms was sold up. The new people don't do rooms. Can't get the labour.'

'Well, what *am* I to do?' The realisation that it was no business of the porter to answer this question made Pendlebury sound childish and petulant.

The porter looked at him. Then he jerked his head as he had done to the guard and began to move away. Picking up his suitcase (the other hand was still numb and disembodied), Pendlebury followed him. Snow was beginning to fall, not in flakes but in single stabbing spots.

The porter went first to a small office, lighted by a sizzling Tilley lamp and heated to stuffiness by a crackling coke stove. Here he silently performed a series of obscure tasks, while Pendlebury waited. Finally he motioned

Pendlebury out, drew the fire, extinguished the light, and locked the door. Then he lifted from its bracket the single oil lamp which illuminated the platform and opened a door marked 'General Waiting Room'. Once more he jerked his head. This time he was holding the light by his dark face, and Pendlebury was startled by the suddenness and violence of the movement. It was a wonder that the porter did not injure his neck.

'Mind you, I'm not taking any responsibility. If you choose to spend the night, it's entirely your own risk.'

'It's not a matter of choice,' rejoined Pendlebury.

'It's against the regulations to use the waiting rooms for any purpose but waiting for the company's trains.'

'They're not the company's trains any more. They're supposed to be *our* trains.'

Presumably the porter had heard that too often to consider it worth reply.

'You can keep the lamp while the oil lasts.'

'Thank you,' said Pendlebury. 'What about a fire?'

'Not since before the war.'

'I see,' said Pendlebury. 'I suppose you're sure there's nowhere else?'

'Have a look if you want to.'

Through the door Pendlebury could see the drops of snow scudding past like icy shrapnel.

'I'll stay here. After all, it's only a few hours.' The responsibilities of the morrow were already ranging themselves around Pendlebury, ready to topple and pounce.

The porter placed the lamp on the polished yellow table.

'Don't forget it's nothing to do with me.'

'If I'm not awake, I suppose someone will call me in time for the six-thirty?'

'Yes,' said the porter. 'You'll be called.'

'Goodnight,' said Pendlebury. 'And thank you.'

The porter neither answered, nor even nodded. Instead he gave that violent twist or jerk of his head. Pendlebury realised that it must be a twitch; perhaps partly voluntary, partly involuntary. Now that he had seen it in the light, its extravagance frightened him. Going, the porter slammed the door sharply; from which Pendlebury deduced also that the lock must be stiff.

As well as the yellow table the waiting room contained four long seats stoutly upholstered in shiny black. Two of these seats were set against the back wall, with the empty fireplace between them; and one against each of the side walls. The seats had backs, but no arms. There were also two objects in hanging frames: one was the address of the local representative of an organisation concerned to protect unmarried women from molestation when away from home; the other a black-and-white photograph of the Old Bailey, described, Pendlebury observed, as the New Central Criminal Court. Faded though the scene now was, the huge blind figure which surmounted the dome still stood out blackly against the pale sky. The streets were empty. The photograph must have been taken at dawn.

Pendlebury's first idea was to move the table to one side, and then bring up one of the long seats so that it stood alongside another, thus making a wider couch for the night. He set the lamp on the floor, and going around to the other end of the table began to pull. The table remained immovable. Supposing this to be owing to its obviously great weight, Pendlebury increased his efforts. He then saw, as the rays of the lantern advanced towards him across the dingy floorboards, that at the bottom of each leg were four L-shaped metal plates, one each side, by which the leg was screwed to the floor. The plates and the screws were dusty and rusty, but solid as a battleship. It was an easy matter to confirm that the four seats were similarly secured. The now extinct company took no risks with its property.

Pendlebury tried to make the best of a single bench, one of the pair divided by the fireplace. But it was both hard and narrow, and curved sharply upwards to its centre. It was even too short, so that Pendlebury found it difficult to dispose of his feet. So cold and uncomfortable was he that he hesitated to put out the sturdy lamp. But in the end he did so. Apart from anything else, Pendlebury found that the light just sufficed to fill the waiting room with dark places which changed their shape and kept him wakeful with speculation. He found also that he was beginning to be obsessed with the minor question of how long the oil would last.

With his left hand steadying the overcoat under his head (most fortunately he had packed a second, country one for use if the weather proved really cold), he turned down the small notched flame with his right; then lifting the lamp from the table, blew it out. Beyond the waiting room it was so dark that the edges of the two windows were indistinct. Indeed the two patches of tenuous foggy greyness seemed to appear and disappear, like the optical illusions found in Christmas crackers. If there was any chance of Pendlebury's eyes 'becoming accustomed to the light', it was now dissipated in drowsiness. Truly Pendlebury was very tired indeed.

Not, of course, that he was able to sleep deeply or unbrokenly. Tired as he was, he slept as all must sleep upon such an unwelcoming couch. Many times he woke, with varying degrees of completeness: sometimes it was a mere half-conscious adjustment of his limbs; twice or thrice a plunging start into full vitality (he noticed that the wind had began to purr and creak in the choked-up chimney); most often it was an intermediate state, a surprisingly cosy awareness of relaxation and irresponsibility, when he felt an extreme disinclination for the night to end and for the agony of having to arise and walk. Pendlebury began to surmise that discomfort, even absurd discomfort, could recede and be surmounted with no effort at all. Almost he rejoiced in his adaptability. He seemed no longer even to be cold. He had read (in the context of polar expedition) that this could be a condition of peculiar danger, a lethal delusion. If so, it seemed also a happy delusion, and Pendlebury was surfeited with reality.

Certainly the wind was rising. Every now and then a large invisible snowflake (the snow seemed no longer to be coming in bullets) slapped against one of the windows like a gobbet of paste; and secret little draughts were beginning to flit even about the solidly built waiting room. At first Pendlebury became aware of them neither by feeling nor by hearing; but before long they were stroking his face and turning his feet to ice (which inconvenience also he proved able to disregard without effort). In a spell of wakefulness, still surprisingly unattended with discomfort, he began to speculate upon the stormy, windswept town which no doubt surrounded the lifeless station; the yeomanry slumbering in their darkened houses, the freezing streets paved with lumpy granite setts, the occasional lover, the rare lawbreaker, both withdrawn into deep doorways. Into such small upland communities until two or three centuries ago wolves had come down at night from the fells when snow was heavy. From these reflections about a place he had never seen, Pendlebury drew a curious contrasting comfort.

Suddenly the wind loosened the soot in the chimney; there was a rustling rumbling fall, which seemed as if it would never end; and Pendlebury's nostrils were stuffed with dust. Horribly reluctant, he dragged himself upwards. Immediately his eyes too were affected. He could see nothing at all; the dim windows were completely gone. Straining for his handkerchief, he felt the soot even on his hands. His clothes must be smothered in it. The air seemed opaque and impossible to breathe. Pendlebury began to cough, each contraction penetrating and remobilising his paralysed limbs. As one sinking into an icepack, he became conscious of deathly cold.

It was as if he would never breathe again. The thickness of the air seemed even to be increasing. The sooty dust was whirling about like a sandstorm, impelled by the draughts which seemed to penetrate the stone walls on all sides. Soon he would be buried beneath it. As even his coughing began to strangle in his throat, Pendlebury plunged towards the door. Immediately he struck the heavy screwed-down table. He stumbled back to his bench. He was sure that within minutes he would be dead.

But gradually he became aware that again there was a light in the waiting room. Although he could not tell when it had passed from imperception to perception, there was the tiniest, faintest red glow, which was slowly but persistently waxing. It came from near the floor, just at the end of Pendlebury's bench. He had to crick his neck in order to see it at all. Soon he realised that of course it was in the fireplace. All this time after the commencement of the war, once again there was a fire. It was just what he wanted, now that he was roused from his happy numbness into the full pain of the cold.

Steadily the fire brightened and sparkled into a genial crepitation of life. Pendlebury watched it grow, and began to feel the new warmth lapping at his fingers and toes. He could see that the air was still thick with black particles, rising and falling between floor and ceiling, and sometimes twisting and darting about as if independently alive. But he had ceased to choke and cough, and was able again to sink his head upon the crumpled makeshift pillow. He stretched his legs as life soaked into them. Lethargy came delightfully back.

He could see now that the dust was thinning all the

time; no doubt settling on the floor and hard, resisting furniture. The fire was glowing ever more strongly; and to Pendlebury it seemed in the end that all the specks of dust had formed themselves into the likeness of living, writhing Byzantine columns, which spiralled their barley-sugar whorls through the very texture of the air. The whorls were rapidly losing density, however, and the rosy air clearing. As the last specks danced and died Pendlebury realised that the waiting room was full of people.

There were six people on the side bench which started near his head; and he believed as many on the corresponding bench at the opposite side of the room. He could not count the number on the other bench, because several more people obscured the view by sitting on the table. Pendlebury could see further shadowy figures on the bench which stood against his own wall the other side of the fireplace. The people were of both sexes and all ages, and garbed in the greatest imaginable variety. They were talking softly but seriously to one another. Those nearest the fire sometimes stretched a casual hand toward the flames, as people seated near to a fire usually do. Indeed, except perhaps for the costume of some of them (one woman wore a splendid evening dress), there was but one thing unusual about these people . . . Pendlebury could not precisely name it. They looked gentle and charming and in every way sympathetic, those who looked rich and those who looked poor. But Pendlebury felt that there was about them some single uncommon thing which, if he could find it, would unite and clarify their various distinctions. Whatever this thing was Pendlebury was certain that it was shared by him with the people in the waiting room, and with few others. He then reflected that naturally he was dreaming.

To realise that one is dreaming is customarily disagreeable, so that one strains to awake. But than this dream Pendlebury wanted nothing better. The unexepected semi-tranquillity he had before at times felt in the comfortless waiting room was now made round and complete. He lay back with a sigh to watch and listen.

On the side bench next to him, with her shoulder by his head, was a pretty girl wearing a black shawl. Pendlebury knew that she was pretty although much of her face was turned away from him as she gazed at the young man seated beside her, whose hand she held. He too had looks in his own way, Pendlebury thought. About both the clothes and the general aspect of the pair was something which recalled a nineteenth-century picture by an Academician. None the less it was instantly apparent that each lived only for the other. Their love was like a magnifying glass between them.

On the near corner of the bench at the other side of the fire sat an imposing old man. He had a bushel of silky white hair, a fine brow, a commanding nose, and the mien of a philosopher king. He sat in silence, but from time to time smiled slightly upon his own thoughts. He too seemed dressed in a past fashion.

Those seated upon the table were unmistakably of today. Though mostly young, they appeared to be old friends, habituated to trusting one another with the truth. They were at the centre of the party, and their animation was greatest. It was to them that Pendlebury most wanted to speak. The longing to communicate with these quiet, happy people soon reached a passionate intensity which Pendlebury had never before known in a dream, but only, very occasionally, upon awaking from one. But now, though warm and physically relaxed, almost indeed disembodied, Pendlebury was unable to move; and the people in the waiting room seemed unaware of his presence. He felt desperately shut out from a party he was compelled to attend.

Slowly but unmistakably the tension of community and sodality waxed among them, as if a loose mesh of threads weaving about between the different individuals was being drawn tighter and closer, further isolating them from the rest of the world, and from Pendlebury: the party was advancing into a communal phantasmagoria, as parties should, but in Pendlebury's experience seldom did; an ombre chinoise of affectionate ease and intensified inner life. Pendlebury so plainly belonged with them. His flooding sensation of identity with them was the most authentic and the most momentous he had ever known. But he was wholly cut off from them; there was, he felt, a bridge which they had crossed and he had not. And they were the select best of the world, from different periods and classes and ages and tempers; the nicest people he had ever known – were it only that he could know them.

And now the handsome woman in evening dress

(Edwardian evening dress, Pendlebury thought, décolleté but polypetalous) was singing, and the rest were hushed to listen. She was singing a drawing-room ballad, of home and love and paradise; elsewhere doubtless absurd, but here sweet and moving, made so in part by her steady mezzo-soprano voice and soft intimate pitch. Pendlebury could see only her pale face and bosom in the firelight, the shadow of her dark hair massed tight on the head above her brow, the glinting and gleaming of the spirit caught within the large jewel at her throat, the upward angle of her chin; but more and more as she sang it was as if a broad knife turned round and round in his heart, scooping it away. And all the time he knew that he had seen her before; and knew also that in dreams there is little hope of capturing such mighty lost memories.

He knew that soon there would be nothing left, and that it was necessary to treasure the moments which remained. The dream was racing away from him like a head of water when the sluice is drawn. He wanted to speak to the people in the waiting room, even inarticulately to cry out to them for rescue; and could feel that the power, hitherto cut off, would soon be once more upon him. But all the time the rocks and debris of common life were ranging themselves before him as the ebbing dream uncovered them more and more. When he could speak, he knew that there was no one to speak to.

In the doorway of the waiting room stood a man with a lantern.

'All right, sir?'

The courtesy suggested that it was not the porter of the previous night.

Pendlebury nodded. Then he turned his face to the wall, out of the lantern's chilly beam.

'All right, sir?' said the man again. He seemed to be sincerely concerned.

Pendlebury, alive again, began to pick his way from lump to lump across the dry but muddy watercourse.

'Thank you. I'm all right.'

He still felt disembodied with stiffness and numbness and cold.

'You know you shouted at me? More like a scream, it was. Not a nice thing to hear in the early morning.' The man was quite friendly.

'I'm sorry. What's the time?'

'Just turned the quarter. There's no need to be sorry. So long as you're all right.'

'I'm frozen. That's all.'

'I've got a cup of tea brewed for you in the office. I found the other's porter's note when I opened up this morning. He didn't ought to have put you in here.'

Pendlebury had forced both his feet to the floor, and was feebly brushing down his coat with his congealed hands.

'There was no choice. I missed my station. I understand there's nowhere else to go.'

'He didn't ought to have put you in here, sir,' repeated the porter.

'You mean the regulations? He warned me about them.'

The porter looked at Pendlebury's dishevelled mass on the hard, dark bench.

'I'll go and pour out that tea.' When he had gone, Pendlebury perceived through the door the first frail foreshadowing of the slow northern dawn.

Soon he was able to follow the porter to the little office. Already the stove was roaring.

'That's better, sir,' said the porter, as Pendlebury sipped the immensely strong liquor.

Pendlebury had begun to shiver, but he turned his head towards the porter and tried to smile.

'Reckon anything's better than a night in Casterton station waiting room for the matter of that,' said the porter. He was leaning against the high desk, with his arms folded and his feet set well apart before the fire. He was a middle-aged man, with grey eyes and the look of one who carried responsibilities.

'I expect I'll survive.'

'I expect you will, sir. But there's some who didn't.'

Pendlebury lowered his cup to the saucer. He felt that his hand was shaking too much for dignity. 'Oh,' he said. 'How was that?'

'More tea, sir?'

'I've half a cup to go yet.'

The porter was regarding him gravely. 'You didn't know that Casterton station's built on the site of the old gaol?'

Pendlebury tried to shake his head.

'The waiting room's on top of the burial ground.'

'The burial ground?'

'That's right, sir. One of the people there is Lily Torelli, the Beautiful Nightingale. Reckon they hadn't much heart in those times, sir. Not when it came to the point.'

Pendlebury said nothing for a long minute. Far away he could hear a train. Then he asked: 'Did the other porter know this?'

'He did, sir. Didn't you notice?'

'Notice what?'

The porter said nothing, but simply imitated the other porter's painful and uncontrollable twitch.

Pendlebury stared. Terror was waxing with the cold sun.

'The other porter used to be a bit too partial to the bottle. One night he spent the night in that waiting room himself.'

'Why do you tell me this?' Suddenly Pendlebury turned from the porter's grey eyes.

'You might want to mention it. If you decide to see a doctor about the trouble yourself.' The porter's voice was full of solicitude but less full of hope. 'Nerves, they say it is. Just nerves.'

The View

As the boat cast off from the landing stage and began to rise and fall in the yellow waters of the Mersey, Carfax recalled *The Last of England*.

The wide, swift river and the tall buildings on both banks, the Liver Building, the Cunard offices, and the huge constructions, mysterious in purpose, which sprang up like indestructible molehills when the Mersey Tunnel forced its way from shore to shore, provided a scale, lacking in an open seascape, by which to set off the smallness of the vessel. Before him the urgent, dangerous-looking stream could be seen suddenly to end and be replaced by the empty ocean: a question mark in the mind. New Brighton Tower, much larger, apparently, then any southern equivalent, stood at the end of the river like the upright of a gateway the other side of which was concealed from Carfax by the super-structure of the boat. In that building, he seemed to re-member, Granville Bantock had contended with popu-lar audiences and the dead weight of past misery which drips like Mersey rain upon the mind of all artists. Car-fax was not the man to live on the beach like Whitman (the very weather of Liverpool discouraged such a thought), or even like Gauguin (the manner of whose death could please no one) on a warm island, but he suspected that his own not unsuccessful career in the Foreign Office had already so sobered and discoloured his imagination that his music and painting, products now of 'spare time' only, would be unlikely to catch that great joy of emancipation which alone, he asserted, made life and art worthy of attention. Carfax always saw all good in terms of 'emancipation': all beauty, all duty. Others had seen the vision, but the slave selves of their past had intervened, making the gorgeous tawdry, the building in strange materials as rapidly failing in beauty, use, and esteem as the human body itself.

'The very dampness of the air does, however, on occasion lend a wonderful depth of colour to the landscape,' Carfax had read in his guide book. The glass through which he glimpsed life as he sailed that morning imparted this rainbow-watery transient clarity of colour, while compressing and encircling with a boundless edge of uncertainty. Hence *The Last of England*: minor masterpiece, he felt, not so much of doomed adventure and hope to be blighted, as of escape unsanguine but compelled.

Through that unexpected consortium of rain, fog, and wind which is the characteristic climate of Merseyside, Carfax watched the fifteen-foot liver birds on top of the great building recede into the driving cloud which is their element. Mythical, yet, in the case of at least one specimen, to be seen stuffed in a Liverpool public building, these creatures ride the seldom-abating storm like human hopes. He remembered that fifteen years ago he had hastened third-class to Liverpool in pursuit of a beautiful vaudeville actress then appearing in that city at the Shakespeare. Passion, he seemed to recall, was then something unable to be left with his cheap synthetic suitcase in the station cloak-room. The boat was beginning to roll to an extent which many of his neighbours seemed to think disagreeable; and Carfax wondered whether unhappiness or nausea tended the faster to produce the other.

By the time they were nearing the Bar Light, terminus of the long double series of buoys which leads vessels from Liverpool towards the fathomless submarine canyon lying concealed north and south down the middle of the Irish Sea, Carfax had discovered the bow of the boat to be uninhabitably gale-swept and also lacking in seats; astern he found the best place which offered, and, sinking into his overcoat, watched the crew as the lightship was passed heave overboard the 'fish' on the end of a line which, turning in the water, records on a dial the distance travelled. It was cold and damp, but not intolerable, or, at least, not physically so. Carfax wondered what a real storm was like: being swept overboard by a wave, seeing a whole life as a vision to be clutched lest worse befall, watching wet clothes being dried before an almost soaked out fire; or the boredom of life in an open boat with strangers, ships' biscuit accompanying horrible corned beef as a diet, the lack of interest among friends who would have to hear the story for unavoidable social and practical reasons.

As England receded, however, into a memory of ill-painted buildings and a line of unhappy faces taken off their guard on the underground railways, Carfax to his surprise began to notice signs suggesting that his fellow voyagers considered the weather to be improving. A speck of glowing ash blew on his face from a newly lighted cigarette; deck chairs began to be dragged clatteringly over his feet from the heap; from across the boat a hot smell reached him of fish and chips and greasy *Liverpool Echo*; a portable wireless began to thrum and pound, its operator varying popular tunes of the type Carfax himself had composed for small sums of money in earlier days, with violent unaimed thrusts into 'the ether', explorations generally ending in an echo of lowest-common-denominator fundamentalism.

'She has no idea how plain she is and of course you can't tell her,' observed a conspicuously unattractive woman of about forty-five to a replica of herself.

'Communism gives the workers something to work *for*,' vehemently asserted a man in a raincoat. His wispy, colourless hair appeared on his prematurely obtruding scalp-line like the last vegetation in the dust bowl.

'So I said I'd give it to her if she promised to have it dyed green,' remarked a round matron to her bored and miserable-looking husband.

'If you'll bring in the orders, I'll look after production. You can leave that to me. I know how to handle the ruddy Government.'

'In the end I had to drag the clothes off her, and she tried to turn quite nasty.' The speaker looked away from the other man, and laughed gloatingly before resuming his former confidential mutter.

'There's no hope for the world but a big revival of *real* Christianity,' said the serious-minded, rather important-looking man. He was apparently addressing a large popular audience. '*Real* Christianity,' he said again with emphasis.

'Look Roland! A porpoise!' said a woman of thirty to her offspring, in the tone of one anxious to guide rather than dominate the child's formative years.

Soon the bell sounded for first luncheon and the group of passengers round Carfax began to break up, some going below, others opening ill-made packages and trying to shield the contents from dispersal in the gusty wind. The gulls, which would have followed the boat round the world were she aiming that far, drew nearer and flew more urgently over the deck. Carfax recalled that fragment of the great and beautiful Sappho according to which the souls of the dead become white gulls in slow flight before a high cliff in the bright sun. He recalled how he had walked one sunny day along Freshwater Down and thought his own soul took flight and drifted warm and lazy and for ever. Wandering along those white and removed cliffs, he had remembered Wagner's inscription on a copy of the Pastoral Symphony presented to Baron von Keudell: 'This day thou shalt be with me in Paradise.'

His drifting thoughts returned to the gulls shrieking and bickering above him: fierce and free and white and light and doomed. 'The pathetic fallacy!' he thought. He was seated facing directly astern, with his back against the cabinwork. 'Sentimentality!' He squirmed in his seat and his eyes settled upon his shoes, their high polish discoloured by Liverpool weather.

'What's wrong with that?' enquired a voice.

A woman had risen from the seat round the corner of the cabin, where before he had distantly observed her reading, and was standing before him. The book was held upside down in her hand. Carfax recognised it as a volume in the *Collected Translations of Voltaire*.

'I'm feeling hungry,' she remarked in a tone so matter-of-fact and commonplace that Carfax ever afterwards wondered whether she had indeed uttered the earlier surprising question: also whether he himself had indeed spoken his thought aloud. 'Could you possibly remember me till I come back?' She removed a stout oilskin coat, placing it on her seat. She was wearing a jacket and trousers, and a simple white shirt. Her head was bare and the fingers holding the book were long and white.

'I shan't forget you,' said Carfax, not quite certain whether the situation required him to rise to his feet. Moreover, was not the other's tone a little peremptory?

'Thank you for your memory.'

She disappeared.

Men are divided into those who know they find women too attractive for their peace of mind or happiness to be long continued; and those who know they would be happier if only they could come to some sort of terms with the intransigent and rather trivial opposite sex. Carfax, who, upon medical advice, was virtually in

flight, came, it will be gathered, into the former category. Finished with women, almost with the world (for
he had very nearly decided to resign his position at
the Foreign Office), and afflicted for several months
now with a loss of appetite so complete and protracted
that he was beginning to fear it would be permanent,
he reflected with weary bitterness upon his folly and
weakness as, ignoring his promise about the seat, he
descended the steps to the ship's dining saloon.

She was seated at a long table by herself in the half-
filled saloon. Grease-spotted stewards sidled rapidly up
and down with small portions of half-cold mutton. She
had removed her jacket and her smooth light hair lay
upon the shoulders of her close-fitting shirt, giving an
effect at once remote and elegant.

She greeted the entrance of Carfax and his request to
be allowed to join her without the slightest feeling for
or against becoming apparent to him. Neither felt impelled to admit cognisance of the several quite empty
tables near them; but their conversation throughout the
meal was more desultory and broken by longer, more
unstrained pauses than is usual between strangers. They
consumed a bottle of claret and, when coffee came, were
quiet and smiling. She produced some Turkish cigar-
ettes in a rather large gold case.

'Do you know the Island very well?' enquired Carfax.

'Better than anybody,' she replied unemphatically.

'I wonder if you could recommend a good hotel? I am
told there are no visitors at this time of year so that one
can get in anywhere. I thought I'd have a look round

before settling where to stay, but perhaps you could advise me?'

'Advice is always dangerous.'

Propelled by the steady breeze of agreeable impulse, Carfax became confidential, as a man does upon his first luncheon with a woman who pleases him.

'I have been very ill.' The breeze of impulse slackened suddenly: then resumed. 'I have been ordered a long holiday. My doctor suggested the Island.'

'That's what comes of living too long among strangers.' He looked up. But her concern seemed real. 'If you've been ill I think you'd really better come and stay at Fleet.' Then after a pause too brief for Carfax to reply, she continued: 'The weather on the Island's irresponsible at this time of the year and there's nothing whatever you can do about it. If you've been ill you won't want to spend all your time in a hotel lounge. You'd become neurotic – like the rest.'

Carfax winced.

'So stay with me instead. Fleet is a big house and you'll never see me if you don't want to.'

Carfax's thoughts were racing, and his spine muscles were stiff and painful. Normally a man of second, third, and fourth thoughts, he, like all habitual vacillators, varied vacillation with occasional gross precipitancy. When decision is required, reflection avails only a few.

He accepted quietly and gratefully.

He paid the bill and they ascended. She drew on her heavy oilskin coat again and they went forward. As they neared the Island, she stood beside him in the bows of the boat, naming to him the mountains, the castles, the steep-sided narrow creeks, the mansions of the great and rich gleaming like palaces of glass in the now bright sun. Round the Island the water was clear and deep, she said; the air clean and strong. She stood there like a pre-Homeric goddess, or Greta Garbo in *Anna Christie*; her oilskin glistening, her hair streaming, her eyes shining, her voice soft but unfailingly distinct: unforgettable. Grief in Carfax began unobserved to shrink and slumber.

Upon the quay, among the mail vans and relatives and few loitering holidaymakers, an expensive car awaited them, attended by a plain but efficient young woman in chauffeur's uniform, who drove like the wind but with the reliability which can only come from a vocation for the work. As they sped through the streets of the capital and beneath the park walls of the mansions encircling it, Carfax felt himself succumbing to the rapture of swift but secure motion. Suddenly, in a minute or two at the most, like great doors opening, his mind relaxed. He became aware of himself for the first time in many months or years. He lost himself and entrancing happiness chilled him like the creeping bursting dawn.

'Do you recall Johnson's definition of happiness? "Driving briskly in a post-chaise with a pretty woman alongside."'

'Johnson was afraid. Like all mortals.'

'Are you never afraid?'

'Oh yes.' She sighed. 'I am not immortal.'

'Are you quite sure you're not?' She looked at him.

'Immortals have no names, or names that no man or woman may utter. Have you a name?'

'I have three names, but you may not utter them. You will hate them all. They are hideous commonplace names of schoolgirls and young brides, and elderly lonely pensioners, and pure women in books. Godparents' names. Goodly names. Useful names which people in shops can spell. I will not tell you what they are. But I will write them down for you.' She opened the volume of Voltaire and beneath the legend FINIS wrote her names on the tailpiece.

The car had been ascending a mountain road, swift as a motor race. Her pencil tailed off down the page as they bumped over the uneven surface. It dropped to the floor. A strong invisible wind poured through the right-hand window as the car reached the ridge. It ruffled Carfax's hair as he stooped to recover her pencil.

'For me,' he said, looking away from her and out at the treeless, houseless, sea-bound plateau, 'you are someone quite different. I shall call you Ariel.'

She could hardly have heard him as he gazed into the unceasing wind flooding through the open window of her car.

'Is the Island uninhabited?' he asked after ten more minutes without sign of smoke or chimney. 'Or, rather, do all the Islanders live in the capital?'

'Only visitors live in the capital,' she answered smiling. Then suddenly she pointed through the window to the sky: 'Look! Geese!' she cried. He could see nothing; nor did the wind or the sound of the car permit of the possibility that the distinctive sound of geese in flight could reach his ears. But Ariel appeared transported with joy. 'How wonderful! The geese have waited to welcome me!' she cried. 'To welcome *us*!' she added, with apology light and heart-warming in her tone. She seized Carfax's arm. 'The geese are the true aboriginals of the Island,' she said in mock seriousness. 'But the visitors come to paint them and catalogue them and protect them, so not many come back now.'

'The white settlers set traps for the native people of Tasmania and soon had them exterminated,' remarked Carfax.

'But the white settlers themselves then fell into the traps,' she replied softly. 'That is why the visitors have to huddle together in the capital. That is why the rest of the Island seems to you uninhabited. You see? Not a building in sight.'

But as she spoke the hills opened and Carfax saw Fleet for the first time.

He found the house hard to place architecturally. Like Inigo Jones's Parliament House in Edinburgh, it was probably older than it looked – possibly much older, for Carfax recollected that he had no knowledge of Island buildings. On the other hand, it might have been a supremely accomplished modern pastiche, weathered to an aspect of misleading age by the Island storms. But a pastiche of what? Of a most beautiful small mansion of the eighteenth century Carfax decided: perhaps the early eighteenth century . . . In any case such speculation was subordinated to wonder at the skill with which the lovely house had been placed in hiding from the world. Carfax had visited Compton Wynyates and marvelled there at the faintly similar effect to that now before him; but the concealment of Fleet was supreme and final, a wonder of imagination and ingenuity, an echo from the deep unconscious.

'How glorious to live there!' Carfax cried with a schoolboy enthusiasm he had never noticed in himself before.

She smiled serenely at him and began to push stray corners of her shirt into the top of her trousers, preparatory to alighting.

'I have never seen anything one half so lovely.'

The car sped up a beautifully firm, even, yellow drive, the gravel rustling sensuously beneath the wheels. Flat, tight lawns called to the spirit on either side and Carfax visualised peacocks. Above the front door something had once been carved, a date, a monogram, a crest, a rebus; but crumbling age or crumbling modern stone-masonry, one or the other, had rendered it now unintelligible. The door was opened by a maid in an elegant grey silk dress. Ariel was momentarily stretching herself upon the step, her oilskin coat a heap at her feet. She was still smiling her small, serene smile. She looked a wonderful quiet happiness.

'Welcome to Fleet!' she said, something in the intonation at once masking and mocking the conventionality of the words.

'Welcome home, madam,' said the grey-clad maid.

*

Carfax's first impression was that the house was full of people. He then perceived that the effect came from several mirrors which reflected and counter-reflected their three figures. These mirrors were not many; but the skilful placing of them gave an effect of magnitude and mystery apparently aided by the construction of the house. Apartments of the most various shapes and sizes led into one another in all directions without doors; and as no two apartments seemed to be decorated alike, the mirrors set up a chiaroscuro of reflections co-existent with but apparently independent of the rich and bewildering chiaroscuro of the apartments themselves. Carfax found he could seldom certainly identify the origin of any particular reflection; and was perpetually troubled by the apparent existence of two separate houses within the space rightly occupied by one. Each room, considered by itself, was perfectly proportioned and exquisitely decorated; but when much of the whole was seen at once, the mind tended slightly to waver and check.

The staircase, which rose before him, passed from side to side of its well, dividing and reuniting at frequent alternate landings: the perfect miniature of a grand staircase on which a duchess receives her guests. Carfax followed the grey-clad maid to his room. As he ascended, he noticed that the constructional principle followed on the ground floor was repeated on the floors above: the same interconnecting undoored rooms, each room different in size, shape, and colour; the same mirrors. The effect was slightly vertiginous: Carfax thought of the three-dimensional chess his divinity tutor had tried to interest him in at Oxford. Also he noticed the stair carpet. A long yellow snake extended its length down the centre of the wide, deep green; the coils of the snake varied in relation to their background, and Carfax, who tended to the obsessive, found himself watching for particular variations to repeat themselves. His room seemed to be on the top floor of the house but he failed to detect a single indisputable repetition in the pattern of the carpet.

At the top of the house the rooms were no longer interconnected and without doors, but the disposition of rooms and corridors was still mysterious and complicated.

The room he had been given was unexpectedly conventional. A white panelled door was set in red-blue wallpaper. A big, old-fashioned brass bedstead, rather French and ornate, set the tone of the furniture: heavy, formerly expensive, never perhaps in the best of taste; very unlike the rest of the house, he thought. The grey-clad maid set down his bag, remarked: 'Tea will be downstairs, sir, when you are ready,' and departed. Carfax crossed to the window and looked out.

Outside was the same empty moorland of the drive in the car, running down to the same clear sea. As they had approached the house, Carfax had considered it to lie in a large dell almost surrounded by fairly high, steep hills. The beautiful wide, empty view now stretched before him, was intoxicating and magnificent; but he found himself completely at a loss to explain whence had come his former strong impression that the house lay uniquely concealed from all the world.

He knelt upon the floor to look in his bag for his field-glasses; and, as he did so, came into that conscious relationship with the pattern and texture of the carpet which begins only with close physical proximity. The carpet, though pleasantly deep-piled, had not, during the brief time he had been in the room, seemed to him otherwise remarkable. But now he noticed that the not unusual pattern appeared, like the snake on the stairs, nowhere to repeat itself. He groped in his mind for the explanation, and before long it came to him that both carpets were possibly pieces of very much larger carpets – of very large carpets indeed, he quickly realised. Reassured by this hypothesis, which related the carpets to the sum total of his life's experience, he briefly examined the view with his strong field-glasses. There was not a house, not a figure, not a road, not a pylon, not even a hedged field: only the ancient sea, the wine-like air. Wagner's words to Baron von Keudell returned to him. This clear, sunny emptiness was what his mind most needed. Deeply content, he put away the field-glasses and descended to tea.

The grey-clad maid was waiting in the hall and took him to a small square drawing-room, where Ariel lay extended on a sofa, a tea-tray by her side. The room appeared to be in an angle of the house, for there were windows in the centres of two adjoining walls; through which, Carfax noticed, the prospect consisted entirely of the near enveloping hills.

'What a beautiful house!' Carfax exclaimed warmly over his bread and butter. 'But you must find it difficult to keep up in these days?'

'We do not have to pay British taxes on the Island,' she replied. 'And everything is much cheaper and better and more abundant.'

'Even domestic servants? Forgive my curiosity. It is only that I am deeply impressed with the beauty of your house. There are no beautiful houses in England now. Only ruins, mental homes, and Government offices.'

'My servants have always been with me,' she answered. 'I do not think they are dissatisfied.'

'I am quite certain they have no reason to be. This place is paradise. Absolute paradise. But people tell me that servants want the pictures nowadays, and there's always the question of what used to be called followers. You seem very isolated here. But I suppose you have lots of visitors, and they bring servants of their own?'

'The people here are not like the English, you know.' She poured him a second cup of tea. 'I have few visitors, but people here have interests of their own and never feel bored.'

'Few visitors in this huge house? I visualised the whole place crowded with them. It all seems in such perfect order, as if every room were awaiting an occupant in the next hour or so. Besides, you yourself—'

'Yes?' Her tone had no flavour of mockery.

'You hardly strike one as living in sequestered solitude on a remote island.'

'I have never said solitude. After all, you yourself are here.'

'I am being foolish. It is because I am so very unused to such dreams coming true as you and your house and my being here.'

'That, I think, is because you fail to draw the essential distinction. I do draw it. You live surrounded by the claims of other people: to your labour when they call it peace, your life when they call it war; to your celibacy when they call you a bachelor, your body when they call you a husband. They tell you where you shall live, what you shall do, and what thoughts are dangerous. Does not some modern Frenchman, exhausted by it all and very naturally, say, "Hell is other people"? But here there are no other people: therefore no war, no marriage, no Government orders, and only such work as you choose and like and Nature herself requires you to do. Here a distinction is drawn. I am surrounded only by my friends – who are not like other people.'

'Am I, then, so unlike other people?' Carfax asked in the schoolboy naivety, new come upon him, which seemed so pleasant to him.

'You are in flight from them!' she exclaimed smiling.

Shortly afterwards she referred briefly to the delights of the house: a carefully selected library, a well-stocked music room with two pianos, a small studio on the roof, a formal garden with a pool. 'And, of course,' she added, 'there's always the Island itself. You can spend a long time exploring that. All your life, in fact. Because the Island's always changing. When Nature's advertising agents say that in books about beauty spots, they are of course trying to conceal what they regard as her frightful sameness and dullness. But here things are different. The Island is never the same and never repeats itself.'

'Or if it does, the pattern is too large for one mortal to comprehend?' interrupted Carfax, thinking of something else. 'Or one lifetime, perhaps?'

'No, I do not think it ever repeats itself,' she answered musing. 'Always there are variations. But, of course,' she added, 'the man in us looks rather for the pattern such as it is, the woman for the variations.' She smiled again. 'But the immediate point is that you won't be seeing much of me during the day, so I do hope you'll find things to do. We are quiet here, but I hope not dull.'

Eagerly he reassured her about both these hopes.

Carfax, who found in her movements a grace he had vainly sought elsewhere, watched her as she rose from the sofa and crossed to the door. She entranced him; so that only a corner of his eye and a fragment of his attention engaged themselves with the figure of what appeared to be a huge and burly man passing first one window and then the other as presumably he walked round the corner of the house. Ariel said nothing: and Carfax, as stated, was entranced by her.

He spent the evening drawing in the garden. The spring sun shone and the surrounding hills protected him from the wind. Immediately he entered the garden his attention had been seized by a certain aspect of these hills: a large landscape of a force and significance utterly unprecedented in his experience clamoured through his brain to be released on to paper or canvas. Without going further he started work, his swiftly moving pencil leaving behind it a line of astonishing power and certainty. It would be a sombre work. In a few hours Carfax had been so far emancipated as to be producing once more and at long last a sombre work ... Even Ariel passed almost from his consciousness as drawing followed drawing and he detached the pages of his block. His pencil travelled as if held by planchette. Tomorrow he would start the final version, the masterpiece. He worked until the gathering cold and damp reminded him that the year was yet young and the Island not a thousand miles from England.

To his astonishment she appeared for dinner in the costume, though simplified, of an Elizabethan man. Dressed in black, and with her white shirt left open at the neck to show her whiter skin, she might have been an actress about to play Hamlet, a Bernhardt or La Verne; were it not that her smooth golden hair hanging on her shoulders made not only her sex but in some way also her authenticity apparent at a first glance. The long black stockings showed off her lovely legs and ensured that every small delightful grace of movement appeared to the greatest advantage.

Carfax asked one question.

'Why do not all women dress like you?' he exclaimed softly. 'To awaken wonder and love?'

'My friends do,' she answered simply, offering him an exquisite little glass.

The small dining-room was oval with a ceiling which, though probably flat, was painted, after the manner of Biagio Rebecca, to appear steeply concave. As they sat at each end of a small oval table in fine satinwood, the grey-clad maid, now changed into evening black, perfectly served the perfect courses.

After dinner they went up to the music room and for hour upon hour played to each other or played duets or played simultaneously upon the two pianos. The maid at intervals brought them coffee and cubes of Rahat Lacoum, placing the trays on the coloured table between them. A fire which had been lighted so illumined the room as to make lamp and candles almost superfluous, especially as both players seemed so well to know the music.

'Who is that bust over the mantelpiece?' asked Carfax.

'I have no idea, absolutely no idea,' she replied. 'He just goes with the house. He is part of the house.'

There were long pauses in their playing as they talked eagerly and softly of the wonders and beauties of music: the hardships and frustrations and irreparable disappointments of the musician. Outside all was still except for an occasional wind which rattled and echoed in flue and window frame. There was no clock and the hours passed, faded, and were lost.

Carfax at last stopped playing and crossed to where she sat at the other piano. She had started to play what she said was an air of the Island: 'arranged by myself'. It curled and dripped through the thickly curtained silence. It seemed without meaning.

Carfax's hands fell upon her black-covered shoulders.

'Oh Ariel,' he said. 'Ariel . . . I love you with all my heart and soul.'

She continued playing the rather thin, even silly, little air. The melody accompanied her reply, spoken slowly and with pauses while she went on playing. She spoke while she softly played, some lines of verse:

'Like the sweet apple which reddens upon the
    topmost bough,
Atop on the topmost twig – which the pluckers
    forgot somehow,
Forgot it not, nay, but got it not, for none could get
    it . . .'

A few more bars and she stopped. Rising a little wearily, she crossed to the small table and, going through the motion of pouring from the coffee pot, demonstrated its exhaustion. She made an indescribable little motion: indicative, it might be, of the bankruptcy also of poesy.

'It must be late,' she said, smiling her steady smile. 'We had better go to bed. We had better go to bed.'

When Carfax returned to his own room in the morning, he found it flooded with sunshine, and swept, to the point of discomfort, by the breeze through the open window. The previous evening upon his return from the garden he had found the shutters and blinds drawn against the oncoming night; so that it was not until now that the contrast once more struck him between the view from his window and the view from outside the house. Now, again seeing the open moorland spread before him, he began to feel an uneasy wonder at the absence, in the view, of those compelling hills which were to be the main feature of his picture. He wondered also at the unwonted lack of method which had accompanied his inattention to the problem while he had been in the garden the day before. But the problem was at once so enormous and, when compared with the other happenings of the previous twenty hours, so small and unimportant, that the mind tended somewhat to reel, at once baffled and bored. Carfax continued, none the less, to stand staring out of the window, half-naked and shivering slightly in the draughts which forced their way round the edges of the now closed sashes.

He resolved at breakfast lightly to besiege the beloved Ariel with some very reasonable questions.

One enquiry answered itself, however, at least in part; for not only did she appear dressed for riding, in breeches and boots, but soon remarked that he would not be seeing her again until the evening. Her attitude, affectionate rather than amorous, seemed in no way influenced by the occurrences of the night; but Carfax's initial disappointment was soon modified by an uprush of feeling, already increasing steadily and rapidly, that whatever she did was the best possible thing to be done, at least from his point of view, the thing most in his own interest. Her doings were mainly mysterious, but seemed to provide him, as well no doubt as her, with odd but complete gratification . . . Now he would have time to get on with his picture . . . He would be able to paint knowing she would return . . . Wonderful fore-knowledge . . . Her daytime activity taking her from him, about which he had been intermittently speculating, appeared to be riding. It sufficed.

'I was wondering,' he said, 'why the very nice room you have given me is so different in style and furnishing from all the other rooms I have seen in the house – from your own, for instance?'

'The house has been built and rebuilt several times,' she answered politely but without displaying much interest in the matter. 'Even on several different sites. And occupied, of course, by many different people. I expect these are the reasons.'

'I thought perhaps my room is in the style of decoration you reserve for your male guests,' he continued, the presence all the time of this thought in his mind and his consequent eagerness to express it impeding his full immediate awareness of her answer.

'No. I draw no decorative distinction between the sexes, my darling,' she replied in the same even tone of slightly patient commonplace. By now, however, something strange in the terms of her earlier answer had passed the resistance necessarily strong in any human mind to such strangeness, and had in part entered Carfax's consciousness.

'You talk the most sweet nonsense, dearest Ariel,' he said. 'And nonsense with a lovely strangeness about it. Lovely nonsense.'

'A very ancient said that all beauty must have something of strangeness,' she replied, again with her serene smile.

'Like your carpets!' he interjected quickly. 'How did you get a stair carpet which is different on every step from every other step? Is it part of a very huge carpet or was it specially made to a design of your own?'

'*Esprit d'escalier*,' she replied, gently smiling. '*Esprit d'escalier*. The answer you cannot make, the pattern you cannot complete – till afterwards it suddenly comes to you – when it is too late.'

'Will it be too late when I know the real answers to my questions?' he asked.

'You must have noticed it is always too late when questions are answered and hopes fulfilled and sacrifices made and murder done. Because it is always later than you think.'

The grey-clad maid brought in a large porcelain bowl heaped with fruit. They ate for a while in the silence of lovers.

Later she rang for the dishes to be removed.

'Don't get painter's cramp or lead poisoning, my darling,' she said as they stood alone in the hall. 'I look forward so much to seeing you alive and well tonight.'

Emotion swept through him and he embraced her passionately. She opened the front door. Outside stood a black horse, beautifully accoutred, the bridle held by the efficient young woman who had driven the car on the previous day. Ariel mounted, smiled at him, and rode swiftly away, the horse's hooves clattering excitingly down the spotless gravel of the drive. Carfax's gaze followed her out of sight. Then, noticing that the efficient young woman seemed to have gone about her business, he proceeded to go about his.

Progress with the wonderful painting proved disappointing. Carfax found himself intermittently re-troubled by the problem of the view. Several times he left his easel and, returning to the house, climbed the serpent staircase to his room for further cogitation and research. Though his knowledge of the technique of orientation was hazy, it seemed clear enough that his room faced south, also that the south front of the house was at his back as he painted; but looking up from the little terrace where his easel stood, he was quite unable either to determine which was the window he had just looked out of or to perceive how any window could possibly offer that wonderful airy panorama. Nor when he looked out from his bedroom could he, owing to the configuration of the house and ground, see his easel; and he had noticed when below that the three parts of the garden, corresponding to the three fronts of the house which did not contain the front door, seemed oddly alike in plan and planting, perhaps identical. In the end he resorted to the familiar device of hanging his towel from his bedroom window (first saturating it with water from his ewer to warrant the absurd procedure in the eyes of any inquisitive cleaner or bed-maker: also tumbling his bed anew, as he thought matters over, in his eagerness for the aspects of the wholly normal);

but when he had descended to the garden he found the soaking object a small heavy heap on the ground and the appropriate window as impossible as ever to detect by any index of open or closed sashes. Irritably he ascended the staircase again (his fifth transit since Ariel's departure), passing once more he noticed, as he had done on each previous occasion, the grey-clad maid, who seemed always so much more in evidence than any other member of the domestic staff.

Back in his room fear rose for the first time to his consciousness as, at the casual glance he had resolved upon, he at once fancied that the view had changed. Sick shivering gripped him as his eyes stared without blinking or moving at a small building, a white-washed cottage of the type a fisherman might be supposed to occupy, which stood at the edge of the distant cliff where Carfax was so certain no building had stood before – no building had stood, in fact, less than ten minutes ago. His whole body was shaking as he sank into a chair and picked up a sheet of some newspaper he had used as packing for a pair of shoes. In the attempt to steady himself he read through the first item his eye lighted upon, though the paper shook so much that reading itself was slow and laboured. It was the report of Our Racing Correspondent upon happenings at Plumpton the day before, now more than a week ago. To Carfax it was all warmth and reassurance; like the aftermath of a bilious attack in school days twenty years before.

He recovered; looked again; felt no fear at all; and decided he had been mistaken. The cottage was still there; but he must have failed to notice it through concentration on the wider view.

He descended once more; once more passing the grey-clad maid, now industriously polishing a suit of armour mounted on the first-floor landing. Something, necessarily something very slight, in the proportions of the armour seemed to him in some way familiar. A flood of feeling swept through him for Ariel who, he at once realised, owing to a lover's inexactitude in such matters, momentarily seemed to him of just that size and (absurdly enough), in some sense, shape and build. Several times already since meeting her he had caught delightful shades and echoes of her loved form and presence where no such things could be except for the infatuate.

He returned to the garden and resolutely began to paint. The notion of further experiments, even of the smallest enquiry, was swept clean from his mind. His tired nerves automatically threw off the slightest trace of conscious anxiety about the view, the only disturbing element in the period of blissful happiness he was now entering upon. Or perhaps very nearly the only disturbing element. For another minor mischief began almost at once to suggest itself: the nearly miraculous concept for his picture had completely disintegrated. Before and after the excellent luncheon the grey-clad maid had provided for him in a little square study well suited to meals taken alone, he struggled and searched to recover what was lost, to produce even a passably good painting. Only daubs and smears and lightning zigzags resulted. A corner of his mind seemed at once to offer the suggestion that in some incomprehensible way, by forcing his thoughts so thoroughly from the mystery of the view he had injured his capacity to paint. Did his imagination in some way have to embrace everything or nothing?

He had heard no sound of Ariel's return but was interrupted by her, returned also to her black Elizabethan costume, as he scratched and fought with lost inspiration. As on the previous evening, night was rapidly descending and he noticed that Ariel was shivering slightly in the sudden chill of the spring evening. It was an enchanting sight. Stretching out his hand, he touched her body between the edges of her deeply open white shirt.

'I love you, Ariel,' he said, 'but I shall never be a great painter.' He indicated the day's several failures.

'I think the secret', she replied, kissing him, 'is to get it down quickly. Quickly. Immediately you see it. When you see it. Don't stop till you've got it down.'

'I wonder how you know? You're perfectly right. Yesterday—'

'That's just it,' she said. 'Yesterday – and today everything's different. Things only exist as long as you see them. And we are all of us nothing but the sum of our moods.'

'Do your moods change very much?' he asked.

'Everything changes. All the time. Very fast. I'm no exception, I'm glad to say. Only the dead fear change. I'm alive, my dear. Really very warm and alive.'

'How long will it be before you change about me?'

'Oh!' The slightly drawn-out ejaculation was enigmatic. 'Shall we go in to dinner?'

He took her arm as a man takes a woman into dinner. From his other hand hung the day's failures, slightly damp with dew or mist.

Every now and then he looked out of his bedroom window and every now and then a new, small, rather distant building seemed to have appeared. One quiet night hour when he awoke without reason while Ariel lay unconscious in his arms, he found himself thinking the ridiculous thought: 'I'm glad I don't have to sleep in that room.' His eye wandered round the warmly curtained walls of Ariel's chamber, the ornate cabinets full of her clothes, the silk-covered furniture; all muffled in darkness save for the patchy starlight from the large opened window. The dimly glimpsed scene, the unique remote creature warm in his arms, composed the utmost possible tranquillity and joy. He forgot about the view in deep surrender to his own released unconscious. By day – after that first day he had seen the first house – his fears were swamped and scattered in sun and wind. But, despite her brief return more than once in conversation to the theme of change, he made no reference to the matter when talking to Ariel, did not risk another of those so natural interrogatives she so lightly made to seem so heavy and unnecessary.

But one morning when he looked at the view for the first time that day, he noticed something nearer the house than the white, and lately multicoloured, buildings on the rather distant cliff edge. At first it seemed as though a big megalith, a rocky pillar of large circumference for a pillar, but medium height, had appeared about midway between the sea and the house. At a second glance, however, what had looked a rock or a work of masonry was seen by Carfax to be a huge, motionless man, immobile and staring before him as if he were indeed a rock or statue; and a man, moreover, whom Carfax at once identified, the man who had walked round the corner of the house during that first afternoon in the angle drawing-room with Ariel. To Carfax it seemed as though all that was fearful concentrated in that enormous figure, unmoving but living, unmistakable though too distant for the clothes or much of the features to be clearly made out; and, as on a past morning, a shudder rose through his body from the foundations of his existence.

The mechanism of protection in his mind was now, however, working vastly better than on the earlier occasion, and association with Ariel had released a thousand springs of compensating happiness in his whole being. Almost at once, therefore, he in great part recovered and was able to go down to breakfast (which Ariel, to his considerable annoyance, apparently never wished to take accompanied by him in bed) without very much embarrassment manifesting in his aspect. None the less, another question was unavoidable.

'One of the Island gods,' she answered. 'Or so they say.'

'Ariel!' he said urgently, his nerves once again

momentarily overmastering him. 'Please tell me. What do these things mean? I am sorry to be so obvious, but I'm a little frightened, dear Ariel. What am I to do? Why does the view from my window change every day?'

'My darling love!' She had risen and seated herself beside him, drawing up a chair. Her arms were round him, her whole nature pouring out in kindness. 'You must remember you've been very ill. You mustn't worry about life. You can't stop things changing. It's useless to try. You mustn't try too much. You remember how upset you were about that picture.' The comforting irrelevant commonplaces made his agitation seem childish and absurd: a neurotic's infantilism.

'Only the commonplace is really comforting, Ariel.'

'Only children, and unhappy people, who are like children, distinguish the commonplace from the exceptional. "Under the common thing the hidden grace." Now you are getting better you are beginning to see within the commonplace the exceptional, to find the exceptional becoming quite commonplace. You have been so long among strangers, my love.'

'But have I been as ill as all that? If things are really so different from what they have always seemed to me, I must have been mad. Mad for years.'

'Quite possibly, my dear,' she replied. 'When you live entirely among madmen, it is difficult to know how sane you are.'

'But I should surely be mad now if I didn't wonder about some of the things that have happened since I've been here? Things I can't understand or find out about.'

'Aren't you happy?'

'I should never before have thought such happiness was possible. At least for me. And it is not that I used to think I knew very much. I used to try to follow Goethe's advice. I tried to worry only about the things I had decided were within the capacity of the mind. One's own mind, or perhaps the best mind that has yet been born, sets the limit of truth. It *is* truth, in fact. Don't you think, Ariel?' He gazed at her anxiously.

'*Cosi e se vi pare*. That is the only truth. And very dull it is. Except perhaps as breakfast chat between people in love.' She rose and resumed eating. 'Metaphysics exist only as the food or the substitute for love.'

'Perhaps it is that the things my mind can grasp here are rather different things from the things it could grasp in England,' he went on hesitantly.

'In England you would have felt guilty for loving me and would be eating a little instead of a lot of butter for breakfast. So things *are* rather different,' she answered lightly. 'There'd be no point in your leaving England if they weren't any different at all.'

'You do *know* that the view from my bedroom window changes every day and sometimes during the day?' he asked desperately.

'It changes and you change with it, my dear. It is your illness which makes you want everything to stay always the same. You are getting better now, quite fast.'

'I can never be perfectly happy, dearest Ariel, until I know why the view from my window changes all the time, and why it is a different view from all the other rooms I have been in, and why – a lot of other things. Why, Ariel, why?' He was pale and anxious. 'If you love me and know the answers, please tell me.'

Real fear for him seemed to appear in her face for the first time. Once more she abandoned her breakfast and stared at him for a moment. 'I don't know the answers, my dear,' she said. 'I don't even understand the questions completely. It only occurs to me that if you were perfectly happy, that too would change. And you would change also and would cease to find it perfect happiness. We can think or do. What else is there? Except that when you and I think and do together there is happiness for a while. I fear if we ask too much we shall lose everything. I am afraid of your questions when we are so happy together.'

Some measure of acceptance began once more to creep over him.

'Ariel,' he said, after a long pause. 'Will you please not ride today? Will you spend the day with me?'

'I shall not ride today,' she answered. Love and not a little fear held them in perfect sympathy.

Rising, she left the oval room. Shortly she reappeared having changed into a striped silk dress and high-heeled shoes. They passed the day doing very little.

Late in the afternoon she offered him another room, which he accepted. He at once moved his few possessions. It was a handsomely decorated apartment, warm and luxurious; and the view from its window was of those steep intractable hills: a view which changed almost too little, Carfax once or twice thought, remembering his struggles to paint it. His love and sleep that night were less than ever troubled by memories of his former bedroom whereat his last glimpse had offered little but peaceful sunshine.

Next day she rode again; but not the day after. The daily habit was broken and henceforth maintained on only perhaps two days out of three. Carfax, baulked of his picture, had taken up work in the music room, where he occupied himself setting some poems written by Ariel herself. Sometimes she would sing the songs to him in the evening. Later he began a larger choral work with words drawn from Beddoes, a handsome hand-printed edition of whose writings he had found in Ariel's library. This composition he seemed never able to complete; but immediately he had started it, he had become aware of a sudden change in his estimate of the earlier songs. Previously he had considered them, especially when sung in Ariel's cello contralto, as the best music he had written. But as soon as he had completed a single day's work on Beddoes, they had seemed to him quite worthless. In the end, he felt seriously ashamed of them and was deterred from actually destroying them only by the fear that Ariel would ask once more to sing them and expose him to the necessity of embarrassingly explaining artistic incompetence and self-derogation. This, however, she never did.

Days and weeks passed without incident seeming to Carfax in any way remarkable save for its content of beauty and happiness. He had put away the songs in his

suitcase; and his struggles with Beddoes, though somewhat unrewarded, were not unpleasurable. Most else
that happened was almost pure joy. Once he reflected
that his mortification about the songs alone exempted
him from that doomed perfection of happiness Ariel had
spoken of. He saw the songs as correspondent to the
flaw reputedly introduced on purpose by the Chinese
into their otherwise perfect works in the hope of thus
diverting the envy of heaven. He mentioned this possibility to Ariel.

'Flaws, my dearest,' she answered, 'are your delight. I
shall dress tonight in odd stockings, to put your mind at
rest.'

So that evening his dinner was shared by a beautiful
court fool, with whom he pleasantly argued whether
Puck or Oberon or (Prospero's) Ariel or even Feste
should be played by man or woman.

One day when she was out riding he came upon a book
he had noticed her reading. Lying spine upwards on a
chair, it brought back to his mind the volume of Voltaire
held open by her fingers when first he saw her. He
found the book to be Dahlmeier's collection of Judeo-
Arabic fables. It was in German, a language he had stud-
ied for Foreign Office purposes, but, like all the other
subjects he had mastered for that reason, had never
since used. His German was now, accordingly, somewhat piecemeal, and the book, moreover, was made no
easier for the unaccustomed by being printed in Gothic
script. None the less, Carfax began to translate to

himself one or two of the fables picked either at random or for their brevity.

The first, so far as he could make out, told of a youth who, on being offered by a sage alternative gifts of Wisdom, Wealth, or Virtue, the gifts losing nothing of impressiveness by their Teutonic initial capitals, selected Wealth. The sage thereupon remarked that the choice proved the youth already had Wisdom as he would now be able to afford Virtue.

Carfax found some trouble in translating the abstract words accurately enough to discern the writer's meaning. But he embarked upon a second fable, which seemed to tell of a youth presented by an afrit (or perhaps the German word did not imply anything so malevolent) with a book of the kind which is read by winding the manuscript from a roller held in the left hand on to a roller held in the right hand. The afrit (if that is what the creature was) explained that whenever the youth felt unhappy or bored he had only to wind the book, which represented his life, a little faster from one roller to the other, and the time would soon pass. Apparently, and as far as Carfax could make out, the manuscript, left alone, would wind itself at the normal pace of the youth's life. Apparently also the youth was not granted the power of protracting moments of bliss by retarding the winding process. The fable went on to describe at some length the youth's life: how he longed for time to pass so that he could be a man, could end his weekly day of fasting, could be with his newest mistress, could hold high office, could be rid of a disease or a duty. And at the end of a life of normal span he proved to have lived for just three months and seventeen days.

The third fable Carfax embarked upon seemed to describe the pleasurable but dangerous activities among a group of warriors of some visitor from another world. This tale contained a number of words completely strange to Carfax (he suspected that no ordinary dictionary would contain them), which, together with the general difficulty the language caused him and the presence of occasionally apprehended suggestions that the narrative might be of exceptional interest, led him to race down the lines, taking in less and less of the sense the faster he read. Soon he realised that the point was altogether lost, so that further progress, at least without a reference book, seemed futile. After examining the binding and the last page (some kind of moral, apparently), he laid the book down as he had found it.

Settling to work upon Beddoes, he found, as he had done before, his mind always a little distracted by the frequency with which that poet seemed to echo his own thoughts and experiences: and particularly thoughts and experiences of which Ariel was at the centre. He remembered the case of the armour on the staircase and a hundred other constantly recurring incidents. The profound and unvarying parallelism between external and internal experience began to seem almost a little morbid. Was he obsessed? With Ariel; or with what else? Was there not a disease of the mind which rendered the sufferer (as in childhood) unable to distinguish between subject and object? Was he receiving hints of his own

183

unbalance? Did that possibly explain much?

The hand which had been lying on the keyboard stopped playing and he realised that he had been striking the same chord again and again. He sat back and reflected. He was not seriously concerned. He did not really believe he was mad: certainly not that his more extravagant experiences since he came to Fleet could be thus explained. He had been very disturbed in mind for several years: quite sufficiently so, he thought, to account for symptoms so minor as those now under immediate consideration; though, on the other hand, hardly more so, perhaps, than almost all his neighbours at home. Ariel, however, had always seemed peculiarly unable to grasp even the existence or occurrence of various things and happenings which had disturbed him profoundly. At first he had thought her unwilling, for some reason of her own, to do so. Now he believed her truly unable. He had on one occasion taken her to the room with the view, and their ideas of what lay visible from the window seemed irreconcilable and deeply disconcerting to both of them. Now he began to wonder whether even the room they were in had seemed alike to them. More and more when occasionally he tried to bring their experiences into harmony or taxed her with enquiries, she seemed truly puzzled as well as merely anxious to comfort an exhausted but much-loved mind. All this, and particularly the outrageous nature of the occurrences themselves, did indeed suggest the possibility of real madness. In one of them: he suddenly thought. He had tried tentative enquiries of the servants; but experienced such difficulty in making his perplexity understood by them that the experiment had proved unavailing. Being used, however, to finding it difficult to communicate with servants, he had not deemed the failure especially notable. With Ariel it came more and more to seem as if in some respects she lived in a world of alien experiences from his; and was herself only slowly coming to realise the fact. Carfax thought of the colour-blind who never find out their idiosyncrasy; of the man who only when adult discovered that one eye had lacked sight since birth. The possibility of complete ultimate harmony between Ariel and him seemed for a moment to suggest some almost sinister opportunities.

He then thought of Ariel's beauty, kindness, varied accomplishments, and apparent deep happiness. If their psyches differed in certain profound and essential respects, she was beyond doubt the favoured one. Might it not be that he was offered, perhaps alone among his unhappy fellow islanders, a wonderful chance of fulfilment? If so, it seemed clear enough that the gift must be taken with some faith and not overmuch investigation. 'Faith!' he exclaimed aloud, as he set himself once more towards Beddoes.

'What's wrong with that?' said a familiar echo. 'Provided, of course, that love is also present.' She had returned and come straight to him in her riding costume. He appeared to have been meditating about things for longer than he had supposed.

*

Although when he first came to Fleet Ariel had spoken enthusiastically of the joys of tramping the Island, Carfax, when he almost immediately afterwards became fully aware of the mystery of the view, had, he now realised, unconsciously resolved that to leave the demesne might be unwise – inimical, he increasingly felt, to his intense but rather precarious happiness. He had never done so; nor had Ariel again made the suggestion. When, therefore, that evening after dinner, she proposed a walk down to the sea, he was concerned.

'Are we not afraid?'

'The Island loves us.'

'Your Island seems different from mine.'

'Perhaps that is because we have never made its acquaintance together.'

They walked down the lawns which edged the yellow drive; through the gates; and along a faint rough track to the cliffs, hand in hand and quite silent. It was now summer. The air seemed warm and cool at the same time, as can only be on small islands. There was no wind and the unpolluted sea lapped and rattled its fetters and spoke in words just unintelligible. They stood on the very cliff edge. Carfax interrupted the silence and the sea with a quotation from 'Dover Beach':

'Ah, love, let us be true
To one another! For the world, which seems
To lie before us like a land of dreams,
So various, so beautiful, so new,
Hath really neither joy, nor love, nor light,

Nor certitude, nor peace, nor help for pain;
And we are here as on a darkling plain
Swept with confused alarums of struggle and flight
Where ignorant armies clash by night.'

She put her arms round him and kissed him. The kiss remained always with him, an agony in the mind: for then the two of them at last met and recognised one another. Later he supposed that this was indeed a moment's perfect happiness for him; but at the time the thought did not occur. Everything but the sea was dark and quiet and timeless. Thought and feeling had stopped and they were immortal. The moment was immortal.

They returned after a while to the house, hand in hand and quite silent. And as their love had begun a little before a quotation, so it ended a little after one: for during the night Carfax, by chance or otherwise, awoke from the deep happy sleep into which, retiring unusually early, they had both fallen after their walk, to find himself alone.

He sought, cried out, and listened. All seemed still in the dark house as he opened the door of Ariel's bedroom and cried: 'Ariel! Ariel!' The volume and precision of the echo rising round those light syllables startled him: and briefly directed his attention away from another mystery that seemed now to be besieging his mind. He groped at once for a light and a key to this new strange impression following Ariel's disappearance. Then, very distant and not loud, he heard several knocks as upon a door. He heard what seemed to be the front door of the house opening and closing and then, he thought, or thought he thought, quick hushed footsteps on the lovely crisp gravel of the drive: but all these experiences through an odd filter of distortion, distance, and unreality, as in some half-waking dreams. He plunged about the mysteriously planned, difficult house, seeking a window which overlooked the drive. All the while he cried: 'Ariel! Ariel!' The other sounds had ceased now; with a finality somehow suggestive of time rather than distance, or of the two mingled, as when a half-dream is lost at full waking. In the end he realised what else was wrong. He was in a different house. He knew at once what house it was; and went to his former bedroom, the unexpectedly conventional room with the red-blue wallpaper and the brass bed, rather French and ornate, in which he had never slept.

As he opened the door, light poured in through the window and a breeze blew out his candle. Looking out at the view for the last time, Carfax saw spread before him on all sides a large town. Skysigns were still flashing and flickering; many of the houses still had lights in the windows, even at that late or early hour. A vague miscellany of noises reached Carfax's ear, for months unaccustomed to the urban pandemonium or garland of sound: a forgotten but unmistakable odour of humanity drifted in on the midnight air. From that smell Fleet had seemed unchallengeably free. As it reached his senses, Carfax knew that he was once more in bondage, irrevocably. A wild, bitter misery at his utter loss descended upon him and clung like the shroud about a man who has been hanged. Never afterwards would he for one waking moment be free from the desperate devouring damned memory of the beautiful creature he had known. He would dream he was with her still or again; and wake to resume his life among strangers. He was past tears, past hope, past appetite, past all but bitter despair at his unequalled loss. He was alone and all the foolish, bad, unlovely world were strangers.

The house was empty and derelict. His possessions proved, when he had closed the window and relighted the candle, to be ranged about the shattered room. He packed and left and walked into the noisy town, still thronged with drunken holidaymakers. He noticed by the gate an estate agent's bill with SOLD affixed diagonally across it in red letters.

Doubtless the house was to be pulled down to make room for villas; or perhaps was to become a private hotel or private school or private asylum. Fleet had at some time been rebuilt on a new site, as Ariel had said: perhaps by some rebellious second son who, inheriting unexpectedly, had seized the chance ruthlessly to make effective his long-standing distaste for the old hidden spot, a spot so hidden that the house seemed almost unborn into time; to that son, no doubt, it seemed unadventurous, unprogressive. Doubtless research at the public library would clear this matter up. But Carfax omitted to go to the public library.

He took the last bus into the capital. He was one of

three or four standing passengers, and, seeing the suit-case he held, a boy rose and offered his seat. Looking for the fare Carfax drew from his pocket a little paper spill which he remembered having found among the pages of Beddoes, where presumably some reader had used it as a bookmark. Sick at heart, he paid his fare, and unrolled the spill. On the inside was written in Ariel's bewitching hand, all freedom and grace, a silly little doggerel verse:

There's nothing in Why
    The question is How?
Whatever you learnt
    From the golden bough.

It was to be supposed that Sir James Frazer's book was in the writer's mind; but there were no capitals. Carfax sank into a motionless misery.

It was only when he entered his room in the big hotel where he spent the rest of the night that the significance struck him of the boy's action on the bus. Before him in the wardrobe mirror as he entered stood an old man, and a few simple tests sufficed to prove the old man to be himself.

He had not slumbered away the years, like Rip Van Winkle in his mountains; but in three months or so he had grown very old.

Next day he took the first boat back to England. Among the huge uniform mass of visitors pushing and thronging the quay now that it was summer, he thought for one moment, as, crowded in on the boat's deck, he glanced up from his unending stupor of misery, that he detected a familiar figure, unusually huge and formidable, standing out one instant in the milling swarm; but recently he had many times caught himself in the act of fancying absurd resemblances, making quite false identifications.

Bind Your Hair

No one seemed able to fathom Clarinda Hartley. She had a small but fastidious flat near Church Street, Kensington; and a responsible job in a large noncommittal commercial organisation. No one who knew her now had ever known her in any other residence or any other job. She entertained a little, never more nor less over the years; went out not infrequently with men; and for her holidays simply disappeared, returning with brief references to foreign parts. No one seemed to know her really well; and in the course of time there came to be wide differences of opinion about her age, and recurrent speculation about her emotional life. The latter topic was not made less urgent by a certain distinction in her appearance, and also in her manner. She was very tall (a great handicap, of course, in the opinion of many) and well-shaped; she had very fair, very fine, very abundant hair, to which plainly she gave much attention; her face had interesting planes (for those who could appreciate them), but also soft curves, which went with her hair. She had a memorable voice: high-pitched, but gentle. She was, in fact, thirty-two. Everyone was greatly surprised when she announced her engagement to Dudley Carstairs.

Or rather it was Carstairs who announced it. He

could not keep it to himself as long as there was anyone within earshot who was ignorant of it; and well might he be elated, because his capture followed a campaign of several years' continuance, and supported by few sweeping advantages. He worked in the same office as Clarinda, and in a not unsatisfactory position for his thirty years; and was in every way a thoroughly presentable person: but even in the office there were a number of others like him, and it would have seemed possible that Clarinda could have further extended her range of choice by going outside.

The weekend after the engagement Dudley arranged for her to spend with him and his parents in Northamptonshire. Mr Carstairs, Senior, had held an important position on the administrative side of the Northampton boot and shoe industry; and when he retired upon a fair pension had settled in a small but comfortable house in one of the remote parts of a county where the remote parts are surprisingly many and extensive. Mr Carstairs had been a pioneer in this particular, because others similarly placed had tended upon retirement to emigrate to the Sussex coast or the New Forest; but his initiative, as often happens in such cases, had been imitated, until the little village in which he had settled was now largely populated by retired industrial executives and portions of their families.

Clarinda would have been grateful for more time in which to adjust herself to Dudley in the capacity of accepted lover; but Dudley somehow did not seem to see himself in that capacity, and to be reluctant in any way to defer Clarinda's full involvement with her new family position. Clarinda, having said yes to what was believed to be the major question, smiled slightly and said yes to the minor.

Mr Carstairs, Senior, met them at Roade station.

'Hullo, Dad.' The two men gazed at one another's shoes, not wanting to embrace and hesitating to shake hands. Mr Carstairs was smiling, benignly expectant. Plainly he was one who considered that life had treated him well. Almost, one believed, he was ready to accept his son's choice of a bride as, for him, joy's crown of joy.

'Dad. This is Clarinda.'

'I *say*, my boy . . .'

Outside the station was a grey Standard, in which Mr Carstairs drove them many miles to the west. Already the sun was sinking. Soon after they arrived they had settled down, with Mrs Carstairs and Dudley's sister Elizabeth, to crumpets in the long winter dusk. Elizabeth had a secretarial position in Leamington, and bicycled there and back every day. All of them were charmed with Clarinda. She exceeded their highest, and perhaps not very confident, hopes.

Clarinda responded to their happy approval of her, and smiled at Dudley's extreme pleasure at being home. An iced cake had been baked for her specially, and she wondered whether these particular gilt-edged cups were in daily use. They neither asked her questions nor talked mainly about themselves: they all made a warm-hearted, not unskilful effort to make her feel completely one with them from the outset. She and Elizabeth discovered a common interest in the theatre (shared only in a lesser degree by Dudley).

'But Leamington's so stuffy that no one's ever made a theatre pay there.'

'Not since the war,' said Mr Carstairs in affectionate qualification.

'Not since the *first* war,' said Elizabeth.

'Is Leamington the nearest town?' asked Clarinda.

'It's the nearest as the crow flies, or as Elizabeth cycles,' said Dudley, 'but it's not the quickest when you're coming from London. Narrow lanes all the way.'

'Fortunately we've got our own friends by now in the village,' said Mrs Carstairs. 'I've asked some of them in for drinks, so that you can meet them at once.'

And indeed, almost immediately the bell rang, and the first of the visitors was upon them. Mr Carstairs went round the room putting on lights and drawing the curtains. Every now and then he gave some jocular direction to Dudley, who was complementarily engaged. A domestic servant of some kind, referred to by Mrs Carstairs as 'our local woman', had removed the remains of tea; and by the time Elizabeth had borne in a tray of drinks, three more visitors had added themselves to the first two.

'Can I help?' Clarinda had said.

'No,' the Carstairs family had replied. 'Certainly not. Not *yet*.'

Altogether there were eleven visitors, only two of whom were under forty. All eleven of them Clarinda liked very much less than she liked the Carstairs family.

Then just as several of them were showing signs of departure, a twelfth arrived; who made a considerable change. A woman of medium height and in early middle age, she had a lined and sallow face, but an alert expression and large, deeply set black eyes. She had untidy, shoulder-length black hair which tended to separate itself into distinct compact strands. Her only make-up appeared to be an exceptionally vivid lipstick, abundantly applied to her large square mouth. She entered in a luxuriant fur coat, but at once cast it off, so that it lay on the floor, and appeared in a black corduroy skirt and a black silk blouse, cut low, and with long tight sleeves. On her feet were heel-less golden slippers.

'I've been so *busy*.' She seized both of Mrs Carstairs's hands. Her voice was very deep and melodious, but marred by a certain hoarseness, or uncertainty of timbre. 'Where is she?'

Mrs Carstairs was smiling amiably as ever; but all conversation in the room had stopped.

'Do go on talking.' The newcomer addressed the party at random. She had now observed Clarinda. 'Introduce me,' she said to Mrs Carstairs, as if her hostess were being a little slow with her duties. 'Or am I too late?' Her sudden quick smile was possibly artificial but certainly bewitching. For a second, various men in the room missed the thread of their resumed conversations.

'Of course you're not too late,' said Mrs Carstairs. Then she made the introduction. 'Clarinda Hartley. Mrs Pagani.'

'Nothing whatever to do with the restaurant,' said Mrs Pagani.

'How do you do?' said Clarinda.

Mrs Pagani had a firm and even but somewhat bony handshake. She was wearing several large rings, with heavy stones in them, and round her neck a big fat locket on a thick golden chain.

By now Mrs Carstairs had brought Mrs Pagani a drink. 'Here's to the future,' said Mrs Pagani, looking into Clarinda's eyes, and as soon as Mrs Carstairs had turned away, drained the glass.

'Thank you,' said Clarinda.

'Do sit down,' said Mrs Pagani, as if the house were hers.

'Thank you,' said Clarinda, falling in with the illusion.

Mrs Pagani stretched out an arm (Clarinda noticed that her arms, in their tight black sleeves, were uncommonly long) and pulled up a chair, upon which she sat. Clarinda noticed also that when she was seated, her hips too looked bony and obtrusive. Altogether Mrs Pagani gave an impression of unusual physical power, only partly concealed by her conventional clothes. It was as if suddenly she might arise and tear down the house.

'You cannot imagine,' said Mrs Pagani, 'how much it means to me to have someone new in the village, especially someone more or less my own age. Or perhaps you can?'

'But I'm not going to *live* here,' said Clarinda, clutching hold of the main point.

'Well, of course not. But there'll be frequent week-ends. Whatever else may be said for or against Dudley, he's devoted to his home.'

Clarinda nodded thoughtfully. She was aware that everyone's eyes were upon them, and realised that Mrs Pagani had so far acknowledged the presence of none of the other guests, well though she must presumably know them.

'Who would want to know any of these people?' enquired Mrs Pagani in a husky, telepathic undertone.

One trouble was that Clarinda rather agreed with her.

'Why do *you* live here?'

'I can't live in towns. And in the country people are the same wherever you go. Most people, I mean. You don't live in the country for the local society.'

Clarinda failed to ask why you did live in the country.

Elizabeth came up with more drinks.

'Hullo, Elizabeth,' said Mrs Pagani.

For some reason Elizabeth went very red.

'Hullo, Mrs Pagani.' She left two drinks with them, and hurried away on her errand of hospitality. Mrs Pagani's eyes followed her for a few seconds. Then she turned back to Clarinda, and said: 'We two will be seeing a lot of one another.'

Again Clarinda could only nod.

'I needn't tell you that you're not what I expected. Do you know where I live?'

Clarinda, still silent, shook her head.

'Have you been round the village yet?'

'No.'

'Not seen the church?'

'It was getting dark when I arrived.'

'I live in the churchyard.' Mrs Pagani suddenly shouted with laughter. 'It always surprises people.' She placed her long bony left hand on Clarinda's knee. 'There used to be a chapel in the churchyard, with a room over it. This is a thinly populated district, and they brought the corpses from the farmhouses and cottages, often a long slow journey, and left the coffin in the chapel waiting for the funeral the next day. And the mourners passed the night upstairs, watching and, of course, drinking. When all this became unnecessary, the chapel fell into ruin. The parish council was glad to sell it to me. The vicar's a hundred and one anyway. I restored it and I live in it. The ground had to be specially deconsecrated for me.' Mrs Pagani removed her hand and picked up her glass. 'Come and see me.' For the second time she toasted Clarinda. 'I call it the Charnel House. Not quite correct, of course: a charnel house is where the dead lie *after* the funeral. But I thought the name rather suited me.' Suddenly her attention was distracted. Without moving her eyes, she inclined her head slightly sideways. 'Just look at Mr Appleby. Used to be managing director of an important company. Appleby's Arterial Bootlaces.'

Clarinda could not see that Mr Appleby, with whom she had been talking before Mrs Pagani's arrival, was doing anything much out of the ordinary. He seemed simply to be telling stories to two or three other guests, who admittedly seemed less interested than he was. But

Clarinda was unaccustomed to making twelve or fifteen intimate acquaintances for life en bloc; and all coming within the, at best, uncertain category of friends' friends.

Again Mrs Pagani had drained her glass. 'I must be going. I only looked in for a minute. I have a lot to do tonight.' She rose and held out her hand. 'Tomorrow then?'

'Thank you very much, but I'm not quite sure. I expect Mr and Mrs Carstairs have some plans for me.'

Mrs Pagani looked her in the eyes, then nodded. 'Yes. You mustn't quarrel with them. That's very important. Well: come if you can.'

'Thank you, I'd like to.'

Mrs Pagani was resuming her expensive sable coat, and saying good-bye to Mrs Carstairs.

'You've nothing to worry about,' Clarinda heard her say, 'Dudley's chosen well.'

'Darling.' It was Dudley standing behind Clarinda's chair. He kissed the top of her head. 'Don't mind her. She's far round the bend, of course, but good-hearted at bottom. Anyway she's the only one of her kind in the village. Pots of money too.'

'What makes you think that, Dudley?' asked the marzipan voice of Mr Appleby. Conversation about Mrs Pagani was now general.

'Couldn't behave as she does if she hadn't, Mr Appleby,' replied Dudley.

That seemed to be the consensus of opinion.

*

When everyone had gone, they listened to the radio. Then they had supper, and Clarinda was permitted, after strenuous application, to participate in the washing up. As they retired in a warm mist of gently affectionate demonstrativeness, the thought crossed Clarinda's mind that she might like to sleep with Dudley. It was still not an urgent wish, only a thought; but in Dudley there was no evidence that it was even a thought. For him the fateful outer wall of the fortress had been successfully battered down after a long siege; the course of time would bring the later degrees of capitulation.

The next morning Clarinda had to admit to herself that she was very depressed. As she lay in bed watching wisps of late-autumn fog drift and swirl past her window, she felt that inside the house was a warm and cosy emptiness in which she was about to be lost. She saw herself, her real self, for ever suspended in blackness, howling in the lonely dark, miserable and unheard; while her other, outer self went smiling through an endless purposeless routine of love for and compliance with a family and a community of friends which, however excellent, were exceedingly unlike her, in some way that she did not fully understand. Elizabeth might bill and coo about the theatre, but it could hardly be said that any one of them had a sense of drama. They lived in the depths of the country, but had no idea of the wilderness. They were constantly together, but knew one another too well to be able to converse. Individuality had been eroded from all of them by the tides of common sentiment. Love me, said Dudley in effect, his eyes softly glowing; love mine. His London personality seemed merely a bait with which to entice her into the capacious family lobster pot. Mrs Pagani was certainly different from the rest of them; but Clarinda was far from sure that Mrs Pagani was her idea of an ally.

Then she got up, turned on the big electric heater, and felt that her thoughts had been the morbid product of lying too long abed. Moreover, the flying swathes of fog were most beautiful. She stood in her nightdress by the window looking at them; with the heater behind her sending ripples of warmth up her back. It was an old sash window with the original well-proportioned glazing bars. The new white paint covered numerous under-currents in the surface of earlier coats. Clarinda liked such details in the house; always kept neat and spruce, like an old dandy whom people still cared about.

But from breakfast onwards her spirits once more began to sink. One trouble was that the Carstairs family, in fact, had no plans for her whatever, and nor had Dudley individually. There was a half-hearted suggestion of church, which no one seemed wishful to keep alive; and after that a sequence of minor interruptions and involved jobs which Clarinda felt could be much better organised, but which everyone else seemed quietly to enjoy as they were. The whole family, Dudley included, seemed to like even the most pointless chores simply because they were being undertaken collectively. The four of them did all they could to give Clarinda a place in the various undertakings; and Clarinda hated the perverse barrier which seemed more and more to isolate her from their kindness. But when by the middle of the afternoon (Sunday luncheon was a substantial reaping of the morning's seedtime) no one had even suggested a walk, she did something precipitate. Without speaking to Dudley, who was helping his father in the garden, she went up to her bedroom, changed into a pair of trousers and a sweater, donned her mackintosh, wrote on the inside of a cigarette box 'Gone for a walk. Back soon', and quietly left the house.

The swathes of fog were still sweeping before the wind, but, though damp, it was not a cold wind nor unfriendly. Immediately she was away from the house, Clarinda felt alive again. After walking a few hundred yards rather furtively, she ascended a roadside bank from which the grass had recently been sickled, and looked about her. She was looking for the church; and when, through a break in the mist, she saw the battlemented top of the yellow stone tower, with a jutting gargoyle at each corner, she knew which way she would go. She turned her back on the church, and walked away from the few cottages which made up the village. Mrs Pagani had possibly served a purpose as serio-comic relief the previous evening, but Clarinda had no wish to enlarge the acquaintanceship.

The patches of cloud and fog drifted and lifted, making constant changes of scene. There was no hope of sunshine, but the mist was uncharged with smoke, and served to melt the sharp air of winter and to enclose Clarinda with an advancing tent of invisibility. Other than Clarinda's light, quick step on the granite chips of the old-fashioned narrow road, the only sound was the dripping of water from the trees, the hedges, the occasional gates. At the tip of every leaf was a fat pearl about to drop and vanish. Clarinda realised that her hair was becoming damp. She bundled it on to the top of her head, soaking her hands in the process; then drew a long black scarf from her mackintosh pocket, and twisted it into a tight turban. The road seemed to be lined with dripping trees, which appeared dimly one at a time, grew into a fullness of detail which had seemed impossible a minute before, and then dissolved away, even from the backward glance; but the air also was itself heavy with soft wetness. Soft and wet, but good on the face . . . 'Let there be wet,' quoted Clarinda to herself in her clear gentle voice. 'Oh let there be wet.'

She had seen no one in the village, and if there were animals in the fields, the mist cut off sight and hearing of them. Clarinda was aware that she might have some difficult personal problems almost immediately ahead of her; but she thought nothing of them as the renewal of contact with the country, the adventurous loneliness of her walk, suffused her with their first freshness. Out of the mist advanced a small square notice-board, lop-sided on top of a sloping wooden pole: 'No Rite of Way,' read Clarinda. 'Persons Proceed Beyond This Point By Favour Only.'

It was perhaps an unusual announcement, and not made more convincing by the misspelling, and by the crudeness of the erection; but Clarinda had heard of landowners who close gates on one day each year in order to prevent the establishment of an easement, and there seemed to be no change whatever in the nature or surface of the road, at least in the short distance ahead which was visible. Clarinda continued her walk.

No one, however, is entirely unaffected, either towards carefulness, or towards challenge, by passing such a notice; and in due course Clarinda realised that she was walking more slowly. Then she perceived that the road itself had for some time been rising slightly but continuously. It also seemed narrower, and the hedges higher. Clarinda stopped and looked at her watch. Despite the muffling mist, she could hear its ticking with extreme clarity, so silent were the hidden pastures around her. It had been something before three o'clock when she had crept out of the house; it was now something after half past. She had possibly another hour of daylight. If she went on for a quarter of that hour, there would be as much time in which to return as she had taken upon the outward journey, and the way back was along a known road, and one which inclined downhill. Moreover, there had not been a single cross-roads or doubtful turning. And in any case Clarinda liked walking in the dark. Certainly neither her mind nor her stomach was inclined to a cosy crumpet tea with the Carstairs family, or to a further session bound, like Catherine upon her wheel, to the mark of interrogation which Dudley remained for her. Again, therefore, she continued her walk.

The gradient increased, but the trees came more quickly, imperceptibly losing, tree by tree, the moment of clear detail which had previously characterised each of them. The road had begun to wind steeply upwards through a wood. Now the hedges, lately so high, had ceased, but the road, although the antique metalling seemed more and more lost in the damp loamy soil, remained distinct. Intermittently, the going had become a little muddy, but the softness underfoot made a change from the angular granite. The trees had now become dim and uniform shapes which passed so quickly and monotonously that sometimes they seemed almost to move, as in a very early cinematograph.

Then, unmistakably, something else was moving. From among the tall, thin trees, and out of the veiling mist, came a small animal. It crossed the track ten or twelve feet in front of Clarinda, and disappeared again almost at once. It neither walked nor ran, but slowly ambled. It was not quite silent, but the atmosphere made the sound of its passage seem insufficient; it whispered and sighed its way through the undergrowth. Clarinda could not think what animal it was. Probably a dog which the mist had misshaped. She checked for a moment, then went on.

Swiftly and momentarily the mist cleared a larger area around her, as she had seen it do several times before. She could see many trees, and could now perceive also that they were beeches. Dotted about the bare earth which surrounds beech trees even in a thick wood were many more of the animals. They were pigs.

Each of the pigs seemed very intent about its business, softly snuffling after unknown sweets in the naked soil. None grunted or squeaked; but the dead, brown-paper leaves rustled slightly as the herd rooted. The pigs were on both sides of the track, and again Clarinda hesitated briefly before advancing through the midst of them.

At first they took no notice of her, perhaps, she thought, unafraid of man because little knowing him; and the tent of mist, temporarily a marquee, advanced with her on to the wooded heights ahead. Then, most unexpectedly, there came from the obscurity thirty yards away on Clarinda's right a shattering animal shriek, short but so loud and high as to pain the ear. All the pigs looked up, stood motionless for a second, then massed together in the direction the sound had come from, some of them crossing the track behind and ahead of her for the purpose. Again they stood, an indistinct agglomeration on the edge of the mist; then suddenly swept back the way they had come. The whole herd, packed tightly together, charged across the track and disappeared into the mist on the left. The pigs had passed no more than five or six feet in front of Clarinda; who was able to observe that in the very middle of the throng was a creature much larger than the rest, a bristling, long-snouted boar, with large curving bluish-white tusks. He it was, she suspected, that had cried from the enveloping mist. She had never before seen such a creature, and was slightly alarmed.

The scampering flight of the pigs could be heard for a few seconds after the fog had surrounded them. Then the wood was silent again. It was as if the pigs had been the last creatures left alive in it. The fog had now closed up again, scudding across the track on a wind which seemed colder and stronger than it had been in the village at the beginning of Clarinda's walk. But the track was now rising steeply, and the extra exertion kept her warm. The long-drawn-out winter dusk must have begun, because not until she was right upon them did Clarinda notice two figures on the path.

They were children. They did not seem to be either ascending or descending, but to be quietly waiting by the side of the track for someone to pass. They were identically dressed in one-piece waterproof garments, like small, trim diving suits, bright blue in colour, and provided with hoods. One child had its hood over its head, but the other was bareheaded and displayed a curly mass of silky flaxen hair, much the colour of Clarinda's own in childhood. The bareheaded child had blue eyes very widely spaced, and a pale skin. The face of the other child was shadowed by its hood, and from Clarinda's altitude amounted to little more than a long red mouth. Both children, Clarinda noticed, had long red mouths. She was unable to determine their sex.

'Excuse me,' said the bareheaded child, very politely. Clarinda decided it was a girl. The girl spoke well.

Clarinda stopped.

The little girl smiled charmingly. 'Have you seen the pigs?' She spoke as if the pigs were a matter of common interest to them, and automatically identifiable; as if a straggler from a hunt had asked, Had she seen the hounds?

'Yes,' said Clarinda. 'Are they your pigs?'

'How long ago?' asked the child, with a child's disregard of side issues.

'About five minutes ago.' Clarinda looked at her watch. Quarter to four. Time to go back. 'As a matter of fact, I'm afraid I frightened them.'

'Silly old pigs,' said the child, fortunately taking Clarinda's side. 'Which way did they go? *This* way? Or *that* way?' She indicated up the hill or down. Clarinda thought that she was about eight.

'That way, I'm afraid,' said Clarinda, pointing vaguely into the mist. 'I hope they'll not get lost in the fog.'

'There's always a fog,' said the child.

Clarinda let that one go.

'What happens if I get to the top?' she asked.

The hooded child, who had said nothing, suddenly made an odd movement. It raised one foot and stamped on the ground. It was as if its whole small body were swept by a spasm. The movement reminded Clarinda of an animal which had been startled and pawed the earth: a large animal, moreover. In the child seemed to be a disproportionate strength. Clarinda was really frightened by it.

'There's a lovely view some days,' said the bareheaded child helpfully.

'Not much good this evening.'

The child shook its head, smiling politely. The hooded child snatched at the bareheaded child's sleeve and pulled it sharply.

'There's a maze.' The bareheaded child was showing

off slightly but meaning to help also.

'What kind of maze? With hedges? I don't believe it.' To Clarinda a maze meant Hampton Court.

'An ordinary maze. You have to look for it though.'

'How far away?'

'Quite near.'

'Where do I look?' Clearly the child was speaking the truth, and Clarinda was interested.

'In among the bushes. There's a little path.'

Clarinda noticed that the second child had cocked up its head and was looking at her. It seemed to have sharp, sallow features, and big eyes. In its hood it was not un-like a falcon.

'Shall I get lost in the maze?'

The bareheaded child appeared unable to understand this question and looked at Clarinda disappointedly.

'Well that's up to me,' said Clarinda, coming to the rescue.

The child nodded. She had still not understood. 'Thank you for telling us about the pigs.'

'Thank you for telling me about the maze.'

The little girl smiled her pretty smile. Really I never saw such a beautiful child, thought Clarinda. The chil-dren departed quickly down the hill. In a moment they had vanished.

Clarinda again looked at her watch. Three-fifty. She decided that she would give fifteen minutes to looking for the child's maze, and that even then she would be back soon after five.

Before long she reached a gate. It was at the edge of

the wood and the end of the track. Outside the wood was short, downlike grass, mossy with moisture. Clarinda's feet sank into it, as into very soft rubber. There were frequent, irregularly placed clumps of thorny scrub, and no sign of even the sketchiest path. The wind was still growing chillier, and the mist was darkening all the time. Clarinda had not gone fifty yards from the gate when she decided to return. The question of whether or not it would be worth looking for the maze did not arise. On top of the hill it would be easy to lose oneself without entering a maze.

In the dim light she perceived that a man was leaning against the gate and facing her. He had red curly hair which had receded slightly at the sides, and a prominent nose. He wore pale-hued riding breeches and dark boots. Across his shoulders was a fur cape, which Clarinda vaguely connected with the idea of aviation. As Clarinda approached, he neither spoke nor moved. She saw that in his right hand he held a long thick shepherd's crook. It was black, and reached from the ground to his shoulder.

Clarinda put her hand on the wooden drawbar of the gate. She assumed that this action would make the man move. But he continued leaning on the gate and regarding her. If she opened the gate, he would fall.

'I want to go through.' It was not an occasion for undue politeness.

Without change of expression, the man swiftly placed his left hand on the other end of the drawbar. Clarinda pushed at it, but it would not give. Not given to panic,

Clarinda momentarily considered the situation, and began to climb the gate.

'*Hullo*,' said a voice behind her. 'Rufo! What do you suppose you're doing?' Unmistakably it was the voice of Mrs Pagani.

Clarinda stepped down. Mrs Pagani was also wearing high boots, and her head was enveloped like Clarinda's in a dark scarf; but, strangely, she was wearing the capacious and opulent fur coat in which Clarinda had first seen her. The top of her boots were hidden beneath it.

'Rufo!' Mrs Pagani spoke to the man by the gate as if she were calling off a foolish and over-demonstrative dog. The man said something in a strange language. It was so unlike any language Clarinda had heard that at first she thought he had a defect in his speech.

Mrs Pagani, however, replied to him in what was presumably the same tongue. In her mouth it sounded less unfamiliar because she lacked his oddly throaty delivery. Clarinda wondered whether this might be Romany.

The man was remonstrating against Mrs Pagani's re-proof. Her reply was curious: she was fluently panto-mimic, and Clarinda could not but gather that Rufo was being told that she, Clarinda, was to be admitted where others were to be denied. The man scowled, and leered, then shuffled off. Although young and apparently strong, he stumbled in his gait and leaned on his crook. There was now very little light, but after he had gone a few paces, he appeared to draw his fur cape high over the back of his head.

'What can you think of Rufo?'

Clarinda often found Mrs Pagani's remarks difficult to answer.

'Will you forgive him? And me?'

'There's nothing to forgive. I didn't know he couldn't speak English.'

'How could you?' Clarinda got the impression that the tone of this was not apologetic, but amicably ironical. Not for the first time she thought that Mrs Pagani implied some understanding between them which did not exist.

'And *will* you come back?'

It was ridiculous. But Mrs Pagani had saved her from a menacing situation, and she had to say something.

'When should I come back?'

'Tonight.' The intonation made it plain that no other time could be in question.

'Here?'

Mrs Pagani said nothing, but dropped her head to one side and smiled.

It was almost impossible after that to seek a reason.

Moreover, Mrs Pagani left no time.

'You've bound your hair very well.'

Clarinda had been noticing how carefully Mrs Pagani's own thick locks had been turbanned.

'It was getting wet.'

Mrs Pagani nodded and smiled. She was looking Clarinda over.

'*Au revoir.*'

Clarinda had not expected that either.

'Good-bye. Thank you for rescuing me.'

'My dear, we wouldn't lose *you*.' Mrs Pagani strode off. The plural was a new mystery, for Clarinda felt that it could not refer to Rufo.

Although by now it was night, Clarinda leaped and ran down the dark track. At one time she thought she heard the pigs softly rooting in the invisible under-growth. But she did not stop to listen, and duly reached the house only a few minutes after five.

Dudley seemed to take her escapade for granted (although she provided no details). Clarinda wondered whether this suggested that already he was growing ac-customed to her, or whether it was evidence that he would be a good and unexacting husband, prepared to allow her due liberty and no questions asked. She cer-tainly valued his success in persuading his family to adopt the same attitude.

'Out at night in winter,' said Mrs Carstairs, 'when you don't have to be!' And upon her gentle mark of ex-clamation, the matter dropped and tea began. Clarinda wondered whether their surprising equanimity was a product of Dudley's leadership in a full discussion dur-ing her absence. She liked Dudley for not fussing, whatever his reasons.

Elizabeth had got out a quantity of clothes and ranged them round the room for inspection and com-parison by Clarinda. This was a lengthy undertaking. In the end there was a knock at the door.

'Liz.' It was Dudley's voice outside.

'One moment.' Elizabeth drew on a sweater. 'Now.'

Dudley entered. 'I've been sent up to fetch you both

214

downstairs.' He smiled fraternally.

'We're ready,' said Elizabeth, looking at Clarinda as woman to woman.

On the dark landing outside, Dudley held Clarinda back for a moment and embraced her. 'Go on, Liz, you fool.' Elizabeth went on. 'You understand?' said Dudley to Clarinda. 'At least I hope you do. I've been trying to keep out of sight as far as possible so that you can get to know the family. That walk of yours. I've been wondering.'

Clarinda squeezed his hand.

'It's all right? And you do like them?'

'Of course it's all right. And I like them very much.'

Every Sunday evening, Clarinda understood, Mr Carstairs read aloud from about half past six until they had supper at eight. Tonight the start had been delayed by her walk and by the discussion in Elizabeth's bedroom; but still there was time for four chapters of *Persuasion*. Mr Carstairs read well, Clarinda thought; and the book was new to her.

Dudley, who could be convincing in such matters, had somehow contrived to arrange that both of them could arrive late at the office the next day: otherwise they would have had to return to London that same night. Soon after supper Elizabeth had disappeared upstairs, saying she had some letters to write, and that she probably would not be coming down again. She bade Clarinda goodnight, and kissed her affectionately on the cheekbone. About half an hour later, Mr and Mrs Carstairs also withdrew. Dudley went to assist his father with stoking up the boiler for the night. The clock struck half past nine. Otherwise the house was very quiet. Clarinda supposed that she and Dudley were being purposefully left to themselves.

'I wish *we* could live in the country,' said Dudley when he reappeared.

'I expect we could.'

'Not the real country. Not unless I get another job.'

'Where does the real country begin?'

'About Berkhamstead. Or perhaps Tring. Nowadays, that is.'

'The country stretches in this direction only.' Clarinda smiled at him.

'For me it does, darling.' She had not yet got into the habit of his calling her 'darling'. 'I *belong* around here.'

'But surely until recently you lived in a town? Northampton is a town isn't it?' She really wasn't quite sure.

'Yes, but I was always out and about.'

Clarinda had observed that every normal English male believes that he wants to live in the country, and said no more.

Dudley talked for some time about the advantages of the arrangement. Then he stopped, and Clarinda perceived that he was waiting for her assent. There was a slight pause.

'Dudley,' said Clarinda. 'How well do your father and mother know Mrs Pagani?'

'Not very well,' said Dudley, faintly disappointed. 'What you would call a bare acquaintanceship. Why?'

'They asked her to the party.'

'Actually they didn't. She heard about it and just came. Not the first time she's done it, either. But you can't put on side in a small village, and she's not a bad old bird really.'

'How do you know?'

'I don't,' said Dudley, grinning at her earnestness. 'So what?'

'What does she do with herself? Live on, I mean?'

'I don't know what she lives on, darling. Little children, I expect, like Red Riding Hood's grandmother. You know she occupies an old ruin in the churchyard?'

'So she told me. I should like to go and see it.'

'What, *now*?'

'Will you come with me?'

'It's a bit late for calls in the country.'

'I'm not suggesting a call. I just want to have a look round.'

'She might think that a trifle nosey, mightn't she?'

Clarinda nodded. 'Of course, you know Mrs Pagani better than I do.' She suddenly remembered a nocturnal stroll in Marseilles with a fellow tourist, who had proved unexpectedly delightful.

'Tell you what I'll do,' said Dudley, 'I'll whistle you round before we push off to Roade tomorrow.'

'We mustn't miss the train.'

'Never missed a train in my life.'

Clarinda's second night was worse than her first, because now she couldn't sleep at all. Dudley had considered that they should go their separate ways soon after eleven, in order, as he said, not to disturb Mr and Mrs Carstairs; and when the church clock, brooding over Mrs Pagani's romantic residence, struck one, Clarinda was still tense and tumultuous in the prickly dark. Without switching on the light she got out of bed and crossed to the window. She hoped that the sudden chill would numb her writhing nerves. When, an hour and a half before, she had drawn back the curtains, and opened the window at top and bottom, she had noticed that the mist seemed at last to have vanished, although it was so black that it was hard to be sure. Now the moon was rising, low and enormous, as if at the horizon the bottom edge of it dragged against the earth, and Clarinda saw that indeed all was clear, the sky starry, and the mist withdrawn to the distant shadowy hills. In the foreground there was nothing to be seen but the silent fields and naked trees.

Swiftly a bat loomed against the night and flew smack against the outer sash. Another two feet higher or two feet lower and he would have been in. Clarinda softly shivered for a moment, then watched the bat skid into invisibility. The silver-gilt autumn night was somehow warmer and more welcoming than Clarinda's unadventurous bed; fellow-bed, twin-bed to a thousand others in a thousand well-ordered houses. The grave self-sufficiency of the night was seeping into Clarinda's bloodstream, renewing her audacity, inflaming her curiosity; and its moonlit beauty agitating her heart. By the light of the big moon she began to dress.

When, upon her return from the woods, she had

taken off her walking shoes, she had thought them very wet; but now they seemed dried, as if by the moon's rays. She opened the door of her room. Again a bat struck the window at the end of the passage outside. There was no other sound but that of disturbed breathing; which, however, seemed all around her. The other occupants of the house slept, but, as it appeared, uneasily. She descended the stairs and creaked into her mackintosh before trying the door. She expected difficulty here, but it opened at a touch. Doubtless it would be side to lock one's doors in a village.

The moon shone on the gate and on the lane beyond; but the long path from the front door was in darkness. With the moon so low the house cast a disproportionate shadow. As Clarinda walked down the narrow strip of paving, a hare scuttered across her feet. She could feel his warmth on her ankles as he nearly tripped her. The gate had a patent catch which had caused her trouble before, and she had to stand for half a minute fumbling.

As she walked along the road, passed the 'By Favour Only' notice, and began to ascend into the wood, she never doubted that at the top of the hill would be some remarkable warrant for her efforts; and she was resolved to find out what it was. Now the regular road-side trees were as clear-cut and trim as a guard of honour, and the owls seemed to be passing a message ahead of her into the thickets. Once or twice, when entering a straighter part of the road, she thought she saw a shambling figure rounding the distant corner ahead, but she decided that it was probably only a shadow.

The bats were everywhere, hurtling in and out of the dark patches, and fluting their strange cries, which Clarinda was always so glad that she was among those who are privileged to hear. There were even some surviving or revitalised moths; and a steadily rising perfume of moisture and decay.

The gate at the hilltop was shut. But as soon as Clarinda drew near, she saw the little blue girl standing by it.

'Hullo.'

'Hullo,' said Clarinda.

'You're rather late.'

'I'm very sorry. I didn't know.'

'It's important to be punctual.' The child spoke in a tone of earnest helpfulness.

'I'll try to remember,' said Clarinda humbly.

The child had opened the gate and was leaning back against the end of it, her chin stuck in her neck and her feet in the ground, holding it for Clarinda.

Clarinda passed through. The moon was now higher, and the soft grass glistened and gleamed. Even in the almost bright light there was no sign of a continuing path.

'I shall get my feet wet.'

'Yes, you will. You should wear boots.' Clarinda observed the legs of the child's blue garment were stuck into close-fitting black wellingtons. Also its hood was now over its head.

There was no sign of the other child.

The little girl had carefully shut the gate. She stood looking ruefully at Clarinda's feet. Then apparently deciding there was nothing to be done about them, she said very politely, 'Shall I show you where you change?'

'Can I change my shoes?' asked Clarinda, humouring her.

'No, I don't think you can change your shoes,' said the child very seriously. 'Only everything else.'

'I don't want to change anything else.'

The child regarded her, all at sea. Then, perhaps considering that she must have misunderstood, said, 'It's over there. Follow me. And do take care of your feet.'

It certainly was very wet, but the grass proved to be tussocky, and Clarinda did her best to keep dry by striding from tussock to tussock in the moonlight.

'Rufo's in there already,' said the child conversationally. 'You see you're the last.'

'I've said I'm sorry.'

'It doesn't matter.' This was uttered with that special magnanimity only found in the very young.

The little girl waded on, and Clarinda struggled after her. There was no sign of anyone else: indeed, the place looked a hilltop of the dead. The lumpy, saturated grass and the rank and stunted vegetation compared most unfavourably with the handsome trees behind.

There was one place where the briars and ragged bushes were particularly dense and abundant, constituting a small prickly copse. Round the outskirts of this copse, the child led the way until Clarinda saw that embedded in its perimeter was a rickety shed. Possibly constructed for some agricultural purpose but long abandoned by its maker, it drooped and sagged into the ground. From it came a penetrating and repugnant odour, like all the bad smells of nature and the stockyard merged together.

'That's it,' said the little girl pointing. They were still some yards off, but the feral odour from the shed was already making Clarinda feel sick.

'I don't think I want to go in there.'

'But you *must*. Rufo's in there. All the others changed long ago.'

Apart from other considerations, the shed seemed too small to house many; and Clarinda could now see that the approach to it was thick with mud, which added its smell to the rest. She was sure that the floor of the shed was muddy almost to the knees.

The child's face was puckered with puzzlement.

'I'm sorry,' said Clarinda, 'but you know I don't want to change at all.'

Clearly she was behaving in quite the wrong way. But the child took a grip on the situation and said, 'Wait here. I'll go and ask.'

'All right,' said Clarinda. 'But I'll wait over there, if you don't mind.' The child seemed not to notice the awful smell, but Clarinda was not going to be the first to mention it.

'*There*,' said the child, pointing to an exact spot. Clarinda took up her stance upon it. 'Mind you don't move.'

'Not if you hurry.' The smell was still very detectable.

'Quite still,' insisted the child.

'Quite still,' said Clarinda.

Swiftly the child ran three times round Clarinda in a large circle. The light was so clear that Clarinda could see the drops of water flying up from her feet.

'*Hurry*,' urged Clarinda; and, the third circle complete, the child darted away round the edge of the copse in the direction from which they had come.

Left alone in the still moonlight, Clarinda wondered whether this were not her great chance to return home to safety and certainty. Then she saw a figure emerging from the dilapidated hut.

The figure walked upright, but otherwise appeared to be a large furry animal, such as a bear or ape. From its distinctive staggering uncertainty of gait, Clarinda would have recognised Rufo, even without the statements of the little girl. Moreover, he was still leaning upon his long crook, which stuck in the mud and had to be dragged out at every step. He too was going back round the edge of the copse, the same way as the child. Although he showed no sign of intending to molest Clarinda, she found him a horrifying sight, and decided upon retreat. Then she became really frightened; because she found she could not move.

The hairy slouching figure drew slowly nearer, and with him came an intensification of the dreadful smell, sweet and putrid and commingled. The animal skin was thick and wrinkled about his neck and almost covered his face, but Clarinda saw his huge nose and expressionless eyes. Then he was past, and the child had reappeared.

'I ran all the way.' Indeed it seemed as if she had

been gone only an instant. 'You're not to bother about changing because it's too late anyway.' Clearly she was repeating words spoken by an adult. 'You're to come at once, although of course you'll have to be hidden. But it's all right,' she added reassuringly. 'There've been people before who've had to be hidden.' She spoke as if the period covered by her words were at least a generation. 'But you'd better be quick.'

Clarinda found that she could move once more. Rufo, moreover, had disappeared from sight.

'Where do I hide?'

'I'll show you. I've often done it.' Again she was showing off slightly. 'Bind your hair.'

'What?'

'Bind your hair. Do be quick.' The little girl was peremptory but not unsympathetic. She was like a mother addressing an unusually slow child she was none the less rather fond of. 'Haven't you got that thing you had before?'

'It was raining then.' But Clarinda in fact had replaced the black scarf in her mackintosh pocket after drying it before the Carstairs' kitchen fire. Now, without knowing why, she drew it out.

'Go *on*.' Clarinda's sluggishness was making the child frantic.

But Clarinda refused to be rattled. With careful grace she went through the moonlit ritual of twisting the scarf round her head and enveloping her abundant soft hair.

The child led her back halfway round the copse to where there was a tiny path between the bushes. This path also was exceedingly muddy; ploughed up, as Clarinda could plainly see, by innumerable hoofmarks.

'I'd better go first,' said the little girl; adding with her customary good manners, 'I'm afraid it's rather spiky.'

It was indeed. The little girl, being little, appeared to advance unscathed; but Clarinda, being tall, found that her clothes were torn to pieces, and her face and hands lacerated. The radiance of the moon had sufficed outside, but in here failed to give warning of the thick tangled briars and rank whipcord suckers. Everywhere was a vapour of ancient cobwebs, clinging and greasy, amid which strange night insects flapped and flopped.

'We're nearly there,' said the little girl. 'You'd better be rather quiet.'

It was impossible to be quiet, and Clarinda was almost in tears with the discomfort.

'*Quieter*,' said the little girl; and Clarinda did not dare to answer back.

The slender muddy trail, matted with half-unearthed roots, wriggled on for another minute or two; and then the little girl whispered, 'Under here.'

She was making a gap in the foliage of a tall round bush. Clarinda pushed in. 'Ssh,' said the little girl.

Inside it was like a small native hut. The foliage hung all round, but there was room to stand up and dry ground beneath the feet.

'Stand on this,' whispered the little girl, pointing to a round, sawn section of tree, about two feet high and four in diameter. 'I call it my fairy dinner table.'

'What about you?'

'I'm all right, thank you. I'm always here.'

Clarinda climbed on to the section of tree, and made a cautious aperture in the boscage before her.

The sight beyond was one which she would not easily forget.

Clearly, to begin with, this was the maze, although Clarinda had never seen or heard of such a maze before. It filled a clearing in the copse about twenty or thirty yards wide and consisted in a labyrinth of little ridges, all about nine inches high. The general pattern of the labyrinth was circular, with involved inner convolutions everywhere, and at some points flourishes curving beyond the main outer boundary, as if they had once erupted like boils or volcanic blow-holes. In the valleys between the ridges, grass grew, but the ridges themselves were trodden bare. At the centre of the maze was a hewn block of stone, which put Clarinda in mind of the Stone of Scone.

Little of this, however, had much immediate significance for Clarinda; because all over the maze, under the moon, writhed and slithered and sprawled the smooth white bodies of men and women. There were scores of them; all apparently well-shaped and comely; all (perhaps for that reason) weirdly impersonal; all recumbent and reptilian, as in a picture Clarinda remembered having seen; all completely and impossibly silent beneath the silent night. Clarinda saw that all round the maze were heaps of furry skins. She then noticed that the heads of all the women were bound in black fillets.

At the points where the coils of the maze surged out beyond the main perimeter were other, different figures. Still wrapped in furs, which distorted and made horrible the outlines of their bodies, they clung together as if locked in death. Down to the maze the ground fell away a few feet from Clarinda's hiding place. Immediately below her was one of these groups, silent as all the rest. By one of the shapeless figures she noticed a long thick staff. Then the figure soundlessly shifted, and the white moonlight fell upon the face of the equally shapeless figure in its arms. The eyes were blank and staring, the nostrils stretched like a running deer, and the red lips not so much parted as drawn back to the gums: but Clarinda recognised the face of Mrs Pagani.

Suddenly there was a rustling in the hiding-place. Though soft, it was the first sound of any kind since Clarinda had looked out on the maze.

'Go away, you silly little boy,' muttered the little girl.

Clarinda looked over her shoulder.

Inside the bower, the moonlight, filtered through the veil of foliage, was dim and deceitful; but she could see the big eyes and bird-of-prey mien of the other child. He was still wearing his bright blue hooded garment; but now the idea occurred to Clarinda that he might not be a child at all, but a well-proportioned dwarf. She looked at the black ground before stepping down from the tree trunk; and instantly he leapt at her. She felt a sharp, indefinite pain in her ankle and saw one of the creature's hands yellow and clawlike where a moonbeam through the hole above fell on the pale wood of the cut tree. Then in the murk the little girl did something which Clarinda could not see at all, and the hand jerked into passivity. The little girl was crying.

Clarinda touched her torn ankle, and stretched her hand into the beam of light. There was duly a mess of blood.

The little girl clutched at Clarinda's wrist. 'Don't let them see,' she whispered beseechingly through her tears. 'Oh please don't let them see.' Then she added with passionate fury, 'He always spoils *everything*. I hate him. I hate him. I hate him.'

Clarinda's ankle hurt badly, and there was palpable danger of blood poisoning, but otherwise the injury was not severe.

'Shall I be all right if I go?'

'Yes. But I think you'd better run.'

'That may not be so easy.'

The little girl seemed desolated with grief.

'Never mind,' said Clarinda. 'And thank you.'

The little girl stopped sobbing for a moment. 'You *will* come back?'

'I don't think so,' said Clarinda.

The sobbing recommenced. It was very quiet and despairing.

'Well,' said Clarinda, 'I'll see.'

'Punctually? That makes all the difference, you know.'

'Of course,' said Clarinda.

The child smiled at her in the faint moonlight. She

was being brave. She was remembering her manners.

'Shall I come with you?'

'No need,' said Clarinda rather hastily.

'I mean to the end of the little path.'

'Still no need,' said Clarinda. 'Thank you again though. Good-bye.'

'Good-bye,' said the little girl. 'Don't forget. Punctual.'

Clarinda crept along the involved muddy path: then she sped across the soft wet sward, which she spotted with her blood; through the gate where she had seen Rufo, and down the hill where she had seen the pigs; past the ill-spelled notice; and home. As she fumbled with the patent catch, the church clock which kept ward over Mrs Pagani's abode struck three. The mist was rising again everywhere; but, in what remained of the moonlight, Clarinda, before entering the house, unwound the black scarf from her head and shook her soft abundant locks.

The question of Mrs Pagani's unusual dwelling-place arose, of course, the next morning, as they hurriedly ate the generously over-large breakfast which Mrs Carstairs, convinced that London meant starvation, pressed upon them.

'Please not,' said Clarinda, her mouth full of golden syrup. She was wearing ankle socks to conceal her careful bandage. 'I just don't want to go.'

The family looked at her; but only Dudley spoke. 'Whatever you wish, darling.'

There was a pause; after which Mr Carstairs remarked that he supposed the good lady would still be in bed anyway.

But here, most unusually, Mr Carstairs was wrong. As Dudley and Clarinda drove away, they saw the back of Mrs Pagani walking towards the church and not a couple of hundred yards from their own gate. She wore high, stout boots, caked with country mud, and an enveloping fur coat against the sharpness of the morning. Her step was springy, and her thick black hair flew in the wind like a dusky gonfalon.

As they overtook her, Dudley slowed. 'Good morning,' he shouted. 'Back to the grindstone.'

Mrs Pagani smiled affectionately.

'Don't be late,' she cried, and kissed her hand to them.

Robert Aickman Remembered

by Ramsey Campbell

'What a self-important, self-regarding so-and-so Aick-man was! Can he really have been as unlikeable as he seems?' Thus Roger Johnson in *Ghosts and Scholars*, issue 25 of that most M. R. Jamesian of journals. He'd been inflamed by a passage Don Herron quoted from a letter from Robert Aickman to Donald Sidney-Fryer: 'I ... cannot pretend that I do not know what you mean when you say that the range of both Henry James and M. R. James is smaller than mine.' Aickman went on to paraphrase the comments he made about M. R. James in his introduction to *The Fourth Fontana Book of Great Ghost Stories*: 'One becomes aware as one reads of the really great man ... all too consciously descending a little, to divert, but also still further to edify, the company.' Nevertheless Robert reprinted 'A School Story', explaining that he found it 'free from this defect. The Provost knew about schoolboys.'

Two points are worth making before I go on: first, that Aickman may only have been more honest than many of us would be if invited to agree that our work was superior to work we didn't particularly admire; second, that we often most dislike in others what we resist admitting about ourselves. Aickman told Sidney-Fryer that he found 'an excessive distancing' in James:

'The reader is not meant to feel too involved. This, needless to say, is an intensely English attitude!' May we assume that Robert was less than happy with the blurbs that compared him to James and praised the 'feline detachment' of *Dark Entries*?

I leave that question unanswered and return to Roger Johnson's. Hugh Lamb responded, 'Definitely not,' and suggested that I might have something to add. Let me gather my reminiscences of Robert into as chronological an order as I can.

I first met him when I was nineteen. Kirby McCauley, as part of the second European trip we took together, had arranged a post-luncheon appointment for us at Robert's rooms in Gower Street. Exactly as Michael Pearson puts it in the publisher's note that introduces Robert's book *The River Runs Uphill*, 'I was acutely conscious of being in the presence of A Great Man.' I was at the peak of my painful shyness with strangers, and may have uttered no more words than were involved in ascertaining whether I might smoke, then a habit of mine. (I was given an ashtray without comment.) At any rate, Kirby did much of the talking, and Robert most of the answering. At this distance I recall very little other than his dainty allusion to the fate of King Zog of Albania.

Ten years passed, and brought the first World Fantasy Convention, where I was among the judges for the World Fantasy Award. I note with sadness that all the nominees for the Life Achievement Award that year – Aickman, Long, Wandrei, Wellman, and the winner, Bloch – are now dead, and recall that the prize for short fiction went to Aickman's 'Pages from a Young Girl's Journal'. I accepted on his behalf, and ferried it back to England to present to him.

He was now living in the Barbican, an apartment complex whose functional exterior concealed, in Robert's case, a home from an altogether more genteel age. He chortled politely at Gahan Wilson's bust of Lovecraft, and served me glasses of cream sherry. (Subsequently he had the bust separated from its stand, and after his death only the base bearing the award plaque was found to have survived. He was, to put it mildly, no admirer of Lovecraft, or indeed of any fiction he regarded as horror.) I must have conquered some of my shyness by then, but I believe Robert helped. Hugh Lamb once rightly said (I may be paraphrasing) that having a conversation with Robert always reminded you how much you yourself knew. Whatever art of conversation has been lost, Robert was one of its masters.

Next year – 1976 – he was guest of honour at the British Fantasy Convention in Birmingham. As the only person there who'd met him, I was made responsible for him. Perhaps by then we knew each other well enough for me to have been able to perceive him as a pale, chubby fellow with the worst teeth I've ever seen in a living mouth. I showed him to his room and returned at the appointed time. He emerged in a suit, not togs generally favoured at conventions even in those bygone days, and declared, 'I am at your disposal.' I introduced him to a number of suitably respectful people, some of whom accompanied my wife Jenny and us to dinner at an Indian restaurant. When the horror writer David A. Riley ('The Satyr's Head', 'The Lurkers in the Abyss') revealed that he'd stood as a candidate for the National Front, Robert quizzed him about Oswald Mosley. Later, a number of us escorted Robert to someone's room-party. I was the first to call it a night, but gather that Robert and Jenny and the anthologist Richard Davis shared a mug for drinking white wine, glasses being scarce. I'm told Robert declared that all men were looking for their Jenny and that I'd found mine.

Next morning he appeared at breakfast in a shirt and sweater. Ken Bulmer approached to tease him about having lightened up, and received a lethal glare. Perhaps Robert was getting himself into an appropriately grave mood to deliver his guest of honour's speech that afternoon. Alas, there is no transcript, but my memory suggests that his talk drew on the philosophy of his Fontana introductions and on the essay he wrote for Gahan Wilson's *First World Fantasy Awards* anthology. Afterwards he admitted disappointment with the audience reaction. 'They don't want standards,' he told me. Presumably his sitting through every item on the programme – something Fantasycon attendees had already ceased to do – confirmed this verdict. To my surprise, of the films shown he preferred *Night of the Living Dead* to *The Leopard Man*, whose reticence and delicacy I would have expected to appeal to him.

By now Robert and I were exchanging letters frequently. 'What a fascinating correspondence we are having!' he wrote. Sadly, I no longer have his letters, which failed to survive moving house, and so I can't re-call if it was just before or just after the convention that I wrote to invite him to stay for a weekend, in our Liverpool house (which is very like George's house in my *The Doll Who Ate His Mother*, including the rabbit).

Either his train was early or I was late. I found him standing outside the barrier and proffered my hand, which he took with, I thought, a brevity close to re-luctance. When I proposed a bus ride home he acceded without demur. Of the ride I remember only asking him (for the purposes of the novel of *Dracula's Daughter* I was about to write') where one might have found fog by the Thames in the era of the tale – Whitechapel? He betrayed no disdain at my lack of research. 'Stepney,' he said at once, and so it was.

We'd invited friends to dine with him: Stan and Marge Nuttall, John Owen. For some reason Robert took a dislike to Marge, even though Jenny formed the view that in general he preferred the company of women. When Marge suggested that the texture of Jenny's chicken tikka might not be authentic he sprang to its defence. Whether this disagreement was the source of the dislike I have no idea, but during a lull in the conversation he asked Marge if she was wearing a wig (which she wasn't, in case the reader wonders). After dinner the conversation focused on artistic mat-ters. Asked his opinion of Iris Murdoch, Robert said only that while it might be too much to expect contem-porary fiction to have uplift, at least it shouldn't take away from life. Rebecca West, he declared, had written the nearest things to masterpieces of literature our century was likely to produce. *Rosemary's Baby* (the novel) he thought 'a good shocker'.

As to films, he enthused about Leni Riefenstahl, *The Blue Light* in particular. *Ugetsu Monogatari* and (later, after I'd commended it to him) *Picnic at Hanging Rock* drew his praise; he agreed that the latter was reminiscent of his own tales, especially (he said) in the scene where the teacher appears in her underwear. A mention of *Don't Look Now* provoked his ire – 'offensive to Du Maurier, to the ghostly and to Venice in particular'. He was contemptuous of Donald Sutherland's accent, which he found calculatedly international, and outraged by Sutherland's sex scene with Julie Christie. When John Owen suggested it might have been put in for commercial reasons, Robert responded with a look that rendered words superfluous. Indeed, dislike often roused his passion; other detestations he expressed while I knew him included the magazine *Private Eye* and the Anthony Shaffer play *Sleuth*.

(Let me return parenthetically to Leni Riefenstahl. In his autobiography *The Attempted Rescue* Robert devotes a chapter ('A Distant Star') to her and cites *The Blue Light* (1932) as his favourite film: 'When it was new I saw it again and again.' It may well have influenced his strange tales, in particular 'The Visiting Star', but his account of the film is stranger still: he has the character of Vigo learning of the blue light when he watches all the men of the village attempt to scale the mountain with ladders, and Vigo later climbs the mountain in their company but

236

reaches the summit alone. In Aickman's version it's Vigo who finds the cave despoiled because 'the villagers have called in experts', and the film ends with him roaming the mountains and vainly calling Junta's name. I don't think any amount of re-editing could change Riefenstahl's film so radically, and must conclude that this vision was to some extent Aickman's own – a vision it conjured up for him, and no less valid for it.)

Sunday gave me time to play him Korngold's early opera *Die tote Stadt*. 'Mr Aickman, you simply must hear it,' a lady had told him, and he was grateful for the chance. At intervals he took out a notebook and made a memorandum, either quoting the libretto or recording an error in translation. Also found worthy of a note was my admission that submitting my 'In the Bag' to the *Times* ghost story competition (judged by Kingsley Amis, Patricia Highsmith and Christopher Lee) had brought me no success. Jenny had the impression that there was something he hadn't forgiven Amis for, perhaps not just for being (as Robert put it) a wine snob. I reflect that they were both in love with Elizabeth Jane Howard. All the same, he vigorously defended the finale of *The Green Man* from her objection that an exorcist had to believe in exorcism for one to work.

Monday found us picnicking in Lancashire, having been driven there by the Nuttalls. Later we visited Chingle Hall near Goosnargh but saw none of the reputed ghosts. Robert felt he and I should sign the visitors' book, and perhaps our autographs still haunt it. On the same trip we failed to find an abandoned waterways terminal Robert had been given to believe was somewhere in the area.

Alas, that was our last meeting. We continued to correspond regularly until he wrote to apologise that he would no longer be able to keep it up, having been told 'not really to my surprise, that I have cancer. At present I am oppressed by the mere vulgar symptoms.' What can one say on such occasions? We assured him he would be welcome to stay whenever he liked, but it's hardly surprising that he neglected to take up the offer. A year or so later he died, leaving me and Jenny with memories we wouldn't be without. Jenny feels he should have given us a sign from the other side by now, since he was such a believer in the supernatural. I'm just as much of a sceptic, and yet I sometimes have a sense of being observed by him, especially if I swear immoderately to myself when there's nobody else to be seen.

So was he as terrible a chap as Roger Johnson thinks? About as much as I am, I'd suggest. I'm the better for having had him as a friend and as an example. Once he commented to Kirby McCauley that there were no longer any vivid men. That was certainly untrue in at least one instance while he was with us.

RAMSEY CAMPBELL *is hailed by the* Oxford Companion to English Literature *as 'Britain's most respected living horror writer'. His novels include* The Doll Who Ate His Mother, The Face That Must Die, The Nameless, Midnight Sun, The Long Lost, The House on Nazareth Hill, Ghosts Know *and* The Kind Folk.